From The Archives of Vidéo Populaire

From The Archives of Vidéo Populaire

Anne Golden

Pedlar Press | St John's

COVER ART anahita azrahimi, 'urban
planning on mercury' (2012, acrylic and
collage on canvas)

DESIGN Zab Design & Typography

TYPEFACE *Cardea* by David Cabianca, Emigre

PRINTED IN CANADA
Coach House Printing, Toronto

LIBRARY AND ARCHIVES CANADA
CATALOGUING IN PUBLICATION

Golden, Anne, 1961-, author
    From the archives of Vidéo Populaire /
    Anne Golden. -- First edition.

ISBN 978-1-897141-75-5 (paperback)

    I. Title.

PS8613.O44F76 2016   C813'.6
    C2015-906392-2

First Edition

ACKNOWLEDGEMENTS
The Publisher wishes to thank the Canada
Council for the Arts and the NL Publishers
Assistance Program, for their generous
support of our publishing program.

À Gabriel

THIS BOOK is the result of original interviews conducted by the author. The words of Maurice Aubert were transcribed by the author from a variety of tape formats, some of them obsolete, sent to her by Mr. Aubert.

From The Archives of Vidéo Populaire

An Oral History

TERRENCE O'MEARA ...on. You probably missed that. Turn. It. On. I want everything I mean everything I say on record, taped. Even this, me talking about not talking, which is ultimately useless. Videotaped, even. That would make sense. You'll see why. If this ever gets off the ground. I know how I seem. I am happy to seem that way, fine, as long as everything I say can be independently verified, played back.

I won't really start until I know the others will talk, too. I'm not worried about Lydia. Of course she will. I need to know the others will. Over the years, I've undertaken lots of things on my own for Vidéo Populaire but this will not be one of them.

LYDIA CARTWRIGHT We've been friends a long time, Terry and I. There is a lot of shit out there about us. I would prefer that the other two speak for themselves about themselves. We can't continue like this, with just the two of us reminiscing and telling our versions. I'm not interested in 'A Partial Oral History of Vidéo Populaire' and you really shouldn't be, either.

TERRENCE O'MEARA Even if you have to use me, go right ahead. Tell them I am the only one talking. If they think it's just me, it might scare them. Well, it might scare one of them. See, I don't mind tricking them, but I also want them to have access to this so that they can hear my suggestions about tricking them. Everything above board.

LYDIA CARTWRIGHT I'm gonna guess that Terry is putting himself forward as the sacrificial lamb. Am I right? I know you can't answer that. Go ahead, sacrifice me, too. I could plant a story with you. I could tell you something that happened, but exaggerate it or skew it. You could let them hear it.

TERRENCE O'MEARA Use machines to convince Maurice. Use videos, too, but not his own, no, really not. I can write you out a list of artists he loves. Or should I read them out? No, I'll write them. I'm not sure at all if any of this will work, but that's what I would do.

LYDIA CARTWRIGHT I would suggest that you tell Maurice he can record his own...interventions. If someone is there, even if it's someone he knows well, he probably wouldn't or couldn't.

TERRENCE O'MEARA Appeal to Carl-Yves by saying that the record would be incomplete. The history will be half-written. Phrases like that. Something along those lines. Do you have access to a Little Red Book? I'm not kidding. I'll loan you mine. Be careful with it, please. It's fragile. Find a phrase in the book that you can adapt into an entreaty for Carl-Yves, something that will hook him into talking. You're smiling now but you will appreciate this later.

LYDIA CARTWRIGHT I would encourage you to do some research, especially because you are approaching Carl-Yves. Terry and the Little Red Book! I have one, of course, but I couldn't tell you where it is. Somewhere in storage.

I didn't know that Terry kept his so close. Cool. And weird. Not sure that would work...a lot of people have moved on from that book, including Terry, so...

TERRENCE O'MEARA Most people who have approached Maurice have been turned away. Maybe not turned away exactly but they have given up because they got no response to phone messages, e-mails or letters. I have sent more than one person over to Maurice's apartment with a note from me, a kind of letter of introduction. This might take a while. How much do you know about video cameras circa 1975?

LYDIA CARTWRIGHT Maurice might. On his own terms, he might. For Carl-Yves, honestly, how would I know? We haven't seen or heard from him since 1982. Terry told me about his suggestions for Carl-Yves and I think they are on the right track. My suggestion is to use Antonio Dutto, a good friend of Carl-Yves's who we all know from the old days. With Antonio, there is no fallout. I know it would not help if Terrence or I got involved. Good luck. I mean that because I would love to see this happen. Oh, wait, I think Isabelle could help. Isabelle Mercier-Lalonde, for Carl.

TERRENCE O'MEARA *On verra c'qu'on verra.* One of Carl-Yves's favourite expressions. *Bonne continuation.* One of my favourite expressions.

LYDIA CARTWRIGHT I'm tired of second-guessing and trying to figure out what could work. There might be names on the lists we gave you that will make Carl-Yves jump in. There are certain people...if he thought they were talking, he might talk. This is all speculation, mind you, as I am basing this on the guy I knew a long time ago.

CARL-YVES DUBÉ This everybody talking, sharing their memories, isn't the equivalent of a jigsaw puzzle, you know, all the pieces fitting together nicely. That would be good, a complete picture, but not possible. Antonio wouldn't leave it alone. He got my wife and kid to convince me. Isabelle talked to me, too.

I want everything on tape, every cough and yawn. Terry always had a tendency to...forget it. I don't want to start that way. I don't remember ever saying 'on verra c'qu'on verra.' Get Maurice. If you get him, okay, we can continue.

MAURICE AUBERT Testing...1, 2, 3.
  jolifanto bambla o falli bambla
  ah comme la neige a neigé
  I remember lots when I press record on video cameras.

TERRENCE O'MEARA I didn't think I would react this way to Carl-Yves' voice...I'm actually really...um, happy I guess. It's like a weight has been lifted off me. I'm so tired of telling this history all by myself. Well, Lydia joins in. I have set phrases...I just find myself repeating the same thing over and over. You get entrenched in these stories and you can't tell anymore. Am I sharing the right stories? It's like it became *my* story.

LYDIA CARTWRIGHT Holy fuck. That's him! What worked? I keep doing that, asking you questions. If you turned off the recorder, would you answer me? I'm good. Let's do it.

TERRENCE O'MEARA Four of us founded an artist-run centre called Vidéo Populaire, VidPop for short, in 1974. The three other founding directors are Maurice Aubert, Lydia Cartwright and Carl-Yves Dubé. When we decided to work together, we had no idea we were founding an artist-run centre. I think we started using that term later on, too...

When VidPop was first up and running, we had the reputation of being very serious, very boring, very political. I used to like surprising people by telling them that VidPop basically happened at a party. I was twenty-three and didn't know what I was going to do with myself. I'd finished my undergrad degree and didn't think I wanted to study anymore. I was working in construction, jobs I could pick up. I didn't have any qualifications or anything like that. I was self-taught or maybe it is more honest to say I learned building and basic carpentry from my father and uncles.

Carl-Yves and I had taken a few of the same classes together, that's how we met, and we went to this party on Sanguinet. Some philosophy teacher from UQAM was giving it. I don't remember his name. I say the party was on Sanguinet but Carl remembers St-Hubert. I think I'm right but the hills are steep on both of those streets below Sherbrooke, so it could have been either.

We met Lydia there that night. She wore her hair long and had these big glasses. Our hair was as long as hers then. She was easy to talk to. She was funny. Until that night I thought Carl-Yves was extremely shy. It kind of dawned on me that he was just reticent. We definitely smoked some pot. We probably had other things, too. Which might account for still being up the next morning, eating bacon and eggs and writing stuff down on a napkin. Lydia took the notes.

LYDIA CARTWRIGHT The napkin. That legendary napkin. Can you imagine if we had known what the napkin would mean? You know all those stories about people who keep a notepad next to their bed? They wake up from this great dream and scribble something down then go back to sleep? In the morning, they read their idea and it says 'orange cat.' The three of us had been up all night at this party and then in a park...other places, too, I think. Then the greasy spoon. We'd been talking politics. I have an image of those two guys devouring plates of food. I'd just met them and we were talking about all these things.

Carl-Yves said he knew some people in New York who had video cameras and were making work. He'd seen some videos there and thought they were amazing. Revolutionary even. There was the New York connection but there were also Canadian and Québec groups. We weren't the first and we weren't the only ones. At first, we thought we would try to get together with other people and buy a camera that we would all be able to use. Then we talked about forming a group. We didn't know anything about registering a name and incorporating or what any of that meant.

As I remember it, we were just talking. I was kind of in the process of realizing what kind of person I was, that I would get taken over by ideas then something else would come along and I'd lose interest. That was a pattern I had. I'd been in Montréal for about a year and a half attending Concordia, which was actually called...um...Sir George Williams University when I enrolled. I was kind of drifting through it. I recall that I was interested in doing theatre. I was also into art history. I was taking piano lessons. I had no clue.

Carl-Yves made the suggestion, I'm pretty sure, that we should think about being a collective, about making it formal without being...too structured. There were examples of other places in the US and Canada and Québec. And Montréal. Vidéographe, of course, the earliest centre. In 1975, there would be Groupe Intervention Vidéo. Vidéo Femmes in Québec City. 1974. Lots of others all across Canada.

I honestly don't remember if that napkin went into my bag or back pocket or if it just got bunched up and thrown out. I don't know that I remember writing on it, but those guys thought I did. It seems to me that we remember that meeting after the party as too charged, too full of details. I don't think we decided quite as much as we think we did.

When we finally met to write out our mandate and founding principals, those guys kept asking me for the fucking napkin. Later on I handed them a grease-stained napkin with some illegible writing on it to kind of up the ante. Carl-Yves tacked it to the wall and would encourage people to read it so they knew the founding principles of VidPop.

You know one of the first things Maurice talked to me about was something about one of his relatives having been at the first-ever film screening. The Lumière Brothers train movie that had people ducking for cover under tables.

I thought that was mythology but Maurice swore it was a family story. I didn't really believe it but pretended to because it seemed important to him. But with Maurice, you kind of never knew. It's so far-fetched it could be true.

TERRENCE O'MEARA Maurice, I call him Moe sometimes, came in a little later, I mean, a little later than the party and the morning after at the restaurant. Carl and I knew him. We had taken an art history course together. I think it was art history. Moe sat at the back and smoked. Everybody did. The teacher, too. You could barely see through the haze. We looked at slides of famous artworks. I wonder sometimes if I actually got a good look through all the smoke.

Moe stopped showing up in class. Probably he thought school was wrong for him. I didn't see him and I realized I was looking for him. Then I saw him in this coffee shop near the campus. I went over and said hi, sat with him. I'm a talker.

MAURICE AUBERT I know where to start. I say that but I don't really so I just will. It began when I was young, maybe eight or nine. I didn't know what I was afraid of but I knew how far I could go from my house before feeling the silver feeling.

I liked what Terry and Carl had to say about starting something. It sounded like I could try something completely new. I liked cameras. I liked Lydia. I could see her clearly.

It was an art history class where we met. Terry. Carl. I really liked that. Oh, very much. I was bummed when someone in the class — maybe Terry will remember this too — someone was wound up because he thought Dadaism was a big joke. He said something like 'those Dadaists are just making fun of us.' It was a big joke in one way but that dim guy would never be able to get it. I mean, Francis Picabia didn't nail a toy monkey to a piece of board for you to feel insulted, *sans-dessin*.

It wasn't a big gesture on my part, not a 'you can't teach me anything' kind of statement, me not showing up for classes anymore. I was already starting to have some trouble. I liked Terry. He was easy to be around. I liked courses about art. The sound a slide projector makes. I miss that. Counting is reliable. Right now I have 793 paper clips in my apartment. It's 43 steps from the machines to the front door.

2" Quad reel-to-reel, 1" reel-to-reel, Sony $3/4$" U-Matic, Sony $1/2$" Betamax. Just a few of the tape formats I've loved. I still use some of them. Poor Betamax.

LYDIA CARTWRIGHT Eventually we had an official founding meeting. We got together a few times informally to talk some more. I remember that this guy Maurice was supposed to show up, but didn't. Tonight for sure. No show. Terry was gung-ho for him. He really liked the guy, his ideas. Carl knew him a bit, too, but I had yet to lay eyes on him. There were doubts. We were at a party and when we got to talking we were carried away. We made a big decision based on a fun evening. But the three of us kept showing up to talk some more.

I don't remember how many times we tried to have a meeting that ended up just being beers and joints at someone's place.

CARL-YVES DUBÉ For a long time I spent all my energy thinking about everything we did, how we did it, why we did it. What our purpose was. Then I spent something like twenty years trying to find a place for all of it, a small-enough space — I saw it as a red box, go figure — that wouldn't blow up in my face if I decided to go down memory lane. It's not that I think the others will leave me out. They are way too honest and decent.

It's so easy to turn things into myth. I remember okay, but not the whole thing obviously. Not all the details. That would be impossible. For that reason, I just want to talk about what I'm sure of. It's important to get this story right but how is that even possible? It's like everything got smoothed over, all the little bumps and some of the big ones, too. That's how memory works. Terrence and I went to this apartment on St-Hubert for a party. I know very well that Terrence's version is that the apartment was on another street. So already the facts are shadowy when you have two people who swear they are both right. Lydia used to say she didn't remember which street it was. We used to joke about it, the street thing, then it turned into an argument. Terrence's version won. Sanguinet is the street, because that's the way he tells it. But I tell it St-Hubert, okay? Maybe we are both wrong. Maybe we should tell it St-Denis.

It seems we were always waiting for Maurice. That never changed much. It bothered me at first then it didn't bother me at all for like five years. At the end, it bothered me again.

One thing I remember clearly was a guy I was friends with, Serge Masson, was interested. He came along to some of the meetings we had before Maurice showed up. I always argued that Serge had as much right to be called a founding member as Maurice. Serge maybe didn't come to THE meeting, the one that Maurice did make it to and that sealed his fate. I used to irritate them all by talking about the *five* founders of Vidéo Populaire.

I did all this research about *lettres patentes* and incorporating a non-profit organization with, of all people, Maurice. Of all people — I say that because he hated stuff like forms and legal documents. I didn't love doing stuff like that either. But he was patient and would pour over those forms. I did the legwork.

TERRENCE O'MEARA Moe was always a little hard to corral. Eventually, he came and we date the founding of VidPop to that meeting, October 2, 1974. In terms of the timeline, the party where Carl-Yves and I met Lydia, that was April 1974. So it took us some time to get it all together. Carl was the big catalyst. I was seeing Maurice regularly on the side, keeping him up to date. There was something about him. I knew he wasn't reluctant or a fuck-up, just not very good socially.

If I remember correctly, Carl was insistent about Serge Masson at first but a little later on he dropped that idea. He dropped him because Masson's politics weren't acceptable to Carl. You know, Lydia and I were always willing to consider Serge as part of the group even though he wasn't at the core but I bet Carl has forgotten that he basically nixed that idea because Serge was not a Marxist. Serge had some bourgeois ideas.

Dan was a friend of mine I met doing construction. Laid back, solid guy. Masson and Carl were volatile together. Dan got along with everyone but ultimately our project wasn't for him. We have a responsibility, I think, to include as many people as can be found. See, we all had close friends who kind of supported us and showed up to help out. Carl wants Serge in, fine. I want Dan. I think Lydia might suggest someone, too.

There were other people, too. People who we talked to and were really interested in our project. I wish I could give a list. I can get a partial list together.

MICHAEL STIRKIN   I dated Lydia Cartwright up until just after the beginning of that video place. Those guys she started hanging out with were these freak types and they had some pretty radical ideas, with which I did not agree. I always thought she got taken in a bit, like a cult or something. I didn't like them and I didn't want her doing it. I wasn't happy. Now I see that my being so mad at her probably pushed her into doing it more. My name was written down on lists there and stuff because I did go to some of those meetings until I couldn't stand it anymore.

MYLÈNE BOISJOLI   I was in *École nationale de théâtre* back when Carl-Yves was my boyfriend. I was used to being the busy one because when you went to École nationale it basically became your life. When he founded Vidéo Populaire with his friends, he became busy, too, and we gradually stopped seeing each other. We even talked about being together again when we had achieved some of our goals. Of course that never happened. We both started shifting and changing. I started going out of Montréal more often to do plays. We kept in touch. He would write me postcards. Sometimes just with a few words on them. At first in the early days of Vidéo Populaire, slogans like *À nous la liberté. Non Pasaran. Serve the People.* I kept them.

LYDIA CARTWRIGHT   Serge Masson barely looked at me. He thought I was only there to take things down, take notes. I remember he even referred to me as 'la secretaire.' It's like he couldn't wrap his brain around the fact that I was part of the group. I was tired of taking shit from guys like that who thought they were so smart, with it, but could really not see a woman without behaving like complete assholes. Speaking of which, my pre-VidPop boyfriend, Michael... I can just guess what Michael will say about me. And what he'll say about the guys. I basically lump him and Serge Masson in the same category.

The big meeting was at my place on St-Zotique. I took the notes again, of course. This time on loose leaf and in long hand. Those papers we kept. The originals are still at VidPop in a plastic protector. I learned my lesson.

It was a funny meeting. Moe was taciturn as ever. But he did say a few things. He loved the idea of video, was really enthusiastic about the technology. Carl-Yves and him bonded about the possible uses of video as a tool for social change. We kept stalling on the name. It was a big thing. You had to get it right, sum up your intentions. Terry came up with it later.

We had no money but we were going to buy a camera, rent an office, furnish it and then see about editing equipment. We weren't naïve, like let's put on a show in the barn, but we didn't realize how much work it would be to get even minimally set up.

SERGE MASSON I didn't think they were going to pull it off. Lydia and Terrence were very different from people I knew. I was from a completely francophone milieu. This was a time when it was still quite rare for francophones and anglophones to mix. And here were these two anglophones speaking French, talking about political things, including the independence of Québec. I had my eyes opened a bit. Oh, Carl and I were friends, but I got the sense pretty quick that to stay friends with him you had to adopt his point of view. I didn't believe in the whole Marxist-Leninist program for Québec. I thought we had to find our own way.

TERRENCE O'MEARA VidPop was formed. That sounds easy. But we still had to come up with our name. Everybody was in agreement that 'video' had to be in there. Vidéo Action, Vidéo Militant were two contenders. Predictably, Carl was for 'militant.' I preferred 'action.' It was Lydia who made the 'populaire' suggestion I'm quite sure. Maurice was not big on the fine points. I don't remember if he had any suggestions. Maybe he just wanted our name to be 'Vidéo.' Once we got through the name, we had so much more to do.

We still had to see about buying a camera and figure out things like an office. My apartment on Brébeuf became the first office. I had a small room I used for storage since there was only one closet in that place.

You think you will remember all the important stuff. Nope. Write it down. That's what I do now. 'Course I keep finding lots of grocery lists. My memory is quite good, but in those days I was kind of like a machine for dates and names. I miss that.

We all had jobs. Some of us had two.

MICHAEL STIRKIN I guess I'm on the list of people to track down and talk to because I didn't stay out of the picture completely. I went to talk to Terry, who seemed like the most reasonable one of those guys and asked him to put in a good word for me with Lydia. I can't believe I did that, but I did. I wanted her back. I sort of tried to get involved but only to see her again but they were just getting things going and I couldn't stand some of their ideas. They were complete commies. That creep Carl-Yves basically told me that I should go because the reason I was hanging around had nothing to do with their cause and that made me bad news. Their first film was going to be about Québec as its own country. So that was it. I wouldn't be associated with that. I couldn't do it, not even to try and talk sense into Lydia. Just look what happened with that one guy who was a friend of theirs who was beaten to death.

LYDIA CARTWRIGHT   I think Terry and I were the ones who had the most to learn in a way. Carl and Maurice knew so much about art. At that point, I was a bit classic in my tastes.

Maurice was all about the Dadaists. There was a spirit of absurdity in Maurice's sense of humour. Not many people know how funny he is because it takes so long to get to know him. He's a huge fan of Francis Picabia. He told me the painting he would most love to have is *L'œil cacodylate*. He would point to a spot in that first office and say 'it would go there.' It was a philosophical thing. He didn't really want to own it. In fact, he thought that owning it would be wrong. He loved the Dadaist and surrealist films. I think him liking Alfred Jarry also made perfect sense. Maurice and Jarry kind of did things backwards or upside down, not to be eccentric, but because they had no choice, that's how they were. We talked about things like that a lot. If I was having a longer conversation with Moe, it had to do with art. He could recite 'Zang Tumb Tumb' by heart. Carl found the Dadaists maybe too frivolous even though they were doing social critiques. Carl liked the Russians, the Constructivists and a few examples of Socialist Realism before that got too obviously repressive.

CARL-YVES DUBÉ   They didn't like my name suggestions for our collective. So we went with something run-of-the-mill but that reflected at least some social engagement, like in *soupe populaire*. Maurice was the one who suggested it. So it wasn't ideal, at least not for me, but I was okay with it. I always despised the abbreviation thing. It removes the political part and I refuse to say it. Also Pop Art is my least favourite.

MAURICE AUBERT The camera was the part that hooked me. Carl and I talked about it non-stop. He talked to people he had met in New York to ask their advice. I had the money so I paid. Then over the next year, they all kicked in their share. I didn't care, but it was important to the others that we all contributed equally.

The silver feeling didn't dissapear or anything. It subsided maybe. It sort of lessened when we had those first cameras in those first spaces.

It was a toss-up between the 1974 Panasonic WV-3085 B/W Vidicon Portapak Camera or the 1974 Sony AVC-3250 Vidicon Small Studio Camera. You had to go to the store and get the salesman to give you the manuals. Then you could see what the cameras looked like. It also depended on what was available. I hadn't really seen a video camera with my own eyes yet so I couldn't visualize it. Now it's easy, go on the web. The store. It was on Ste-Catherine. It was yellow and black. We found it just in time because we were about to drive to the States to look at cameras there.

I would still like a Sony Portapak for my own collection. I was looking on web sites to purchase one, sending e-mails to old-timer video geeks. The lowest price I could find was still a lot. I asked Terry if I could borrow VidPop's and he said of course, anytime. It's a thing of beauty, so simple and pure. It does one thing. One thing.

Oh, but the camera I really would like to have is the TK-204 Solid State from Televue. It looks like a giant whisky flask.

The Lumière story is everyone's. That's what I think. The first film screening in Paris. My great-grandparents were French and they lived in Paris at that time so it's possible they were there. I don't have proof but I always felt linked to that film *L'arrivée d'un train en gare de La Ciotat*. The train is beautiful. Before it arrives from the background, you can see a guy on the other side of the tracks. For just a few frames. I wonder about him. He watches the train and turns slightly to follow it just as it blocks him out of one of the most important films ever. He's watching the machine that is going to turn him into just some guy. I wonder if he saw himself in the movie? Did he go around saying 'I'm that guy in *L'arrivée*'?

LYDIA CARTWRIGHT It's great to have facts. I think back on that time and I have a few facts and images that I think are indisputable. But I'll talk to Terry or Maurice or some other old-timer and they say something that resonates and suddenly I'm questioning what it is I remember.

Believe me, I don't trust my memory and it isn't because it is less sharp. I think we can all agree that talking about something that happened forty years ago is kind of fraught. There were a lot of people around us in 1974. It's like I can't sift through them all to see who was important to the formation of VidPop. Names stand out and Terry and Maurice are on the same bandwagon. There was Pierre Nadeau, Antonio Dutto, Rosemary Drummond. David Summerville, but he came a little later. I remember talking to this guy on the metro about what we were doing. Quite vivid, this memory. His shirt was peacock blue. Or maybe green. See? Did he come by the office? Did I know him from somewhere, or was he a friend of Carl-Yves's? No idea. I mean, it was us four but there was Serge Masson even though I would rather erase him. And did I erase him from some important areas because he irritated me so much? Michael, too. He was kind of vaguely around at the very start. It really pisses me off that he came to a meeting or two, got his name written down because he was present and then he's part of this history. Because basically Terry and Carl told him to go and leave me alone. Of course, I had said exactly the same thing to him, but he wouldn't listen to me. And then there is someone like Laurent Simard. He was probably as involved as Serge or Michael, but so much more important, at least in my eyes.

TERRENCE O'MEARA   Laurent Simard was another guy hanging around in the very beginning. I think he may have found VidPop on his own. Some people did. And he might have, because he was an artist hanging out with other artists.

Laurent was great most of the time. He was also a little iffy sometimes. We even had talks about what to do because he was unpredictable and came around quite often. It was mostly the fact that he could be quite high. We weren't sure high on what, but Carl thought PCP. We were certainly not going to be the ones to condemn someone for doing drugs. He had a charisma like I've never seen. Lydia said something to the effect that the four of us were pretty visible and hardly shrinking violets but compared to Laurent...

Laurent didn't show up for a stretch. He was working with Carl and Maurice on a production. We all hoped he was taking a break from drugs or maybe trying to go off them. Carl came rushing in to VidPop with *Allô police* or *Journal de Montréal*. There was something in the papers about Laurent. He was dead. Killed. We couldn't believe it. One of the things I remember was that our phone barely rang in that first while. When it rang, I would jump and the others would laugh. We had a rotary dial phone. It was loud. The phone started ringing and ringing when the news about Laurent spread. The cops show up at VidPop, because Laurent was connected to Vidéo Populaire.

CARL-YVES DUBÉ   There were a lot of rumours and of course people got things completely wrong. The cops showed up, first uniforms for routine questions. Maybe the next day plainclothes showed up. We stopped answering the phone because we didn't know anything. Also, some people were calling to tell us they thought we were involved. The four of us were all there at the office when the cops showed up again. We had the Che poster, the Marx poster, the Mao poster. We had slogans from the Spanish Civil War written on the wall. We had posters and flyers for political rallies and events plastered everywhere. We had two detectives in suits looking at us like we were guilty of I guess just about everything you could think of. And Laurent was dead. They had the Vidéo Populaire business card in a baggie and kept waving it around. On the back of the card was my name, handwritten, and Maurice's, too. We told them over and over again why Laurent had our card, what he was to us. That was depressing. What he was to us was a sometime pain in the ass who sometimes got it together to help out on a video. Those cops didn't understand what we did at all. Laurent was a writer, essentially. He had notebooks that he was always writing in. Only later did everyone get to know what a great writer he was.

PIERRE NADEAU   Laurent was one of those people you would have wanted to save if you'd had all the information and a time machine. We were all misbehaving back then, most of us. Although the VidPop main drug of choice was pot. And beer. Laurent was an electric guy. He could be a handful, sure, but he was a kick. Maurice didn't drink much but when he did he was a cocktail guy. He made...what were those things called...Old Fashioneds.

MAURICE AUBERT   Laurent sat with me sometimes in the edit suite. He made suggestions. I think he taught me some things just by hanging out. I wish he had made more videos. He wrote. He liked Poe. We bonded on the Dadaists. He liked Hugo Ball best. I asked him if he would recite *Karawane* and if I could tape him doing it.

I was terrified they were going to take us down to a police station for questioning, you know those small rooms with no windows. I felt bad about being scared because I don't like enclosed spaces, but I was still alive. Laurent was gone. Carl and I saw Laurent at VidPop two days before...I always thought we were maybe serious suspects but Carl said no, if we had been we would have known it.

I started to really feel it then. The unease that was outside me was kind of inside, too, and I could see it clearly.

LYDIA CARTWRIGHT There were always rumours that we were being watched by the cops or worse, because we were visible at marches and demos and such. Especially in the beginning. The whole Laurent Simard case kind of put the rumour mill into overdrive. I would hear all kinds of things. I heard things even ten years after Laurent's death. Things like Carl and Laurent always had disagreements and Carl fit the profile for someone who could beat someone up so badly they would die. Or Laurent had something on VidPop, some dark secret and Carl took care of him. Carl and Laurent didn't argue. Carl may have asked him to leave if he was disruptive. But he didn't like doing it. Carl thought Laurent was brilliant. Carl did not have a lot of time for people he didn't like. He had lots of time for Laurent. The worst story was about Maurice, that his mental health suffered because he couldn't deal with the guilt of killing Laurent. Absolute nonsense, but it kind of cast a shadow. Carl was quick to clear people out if they weren't involved in a way he thought was productive.

TERRENCE O'MEARA Carl put up one of his signs on the door to VidPop. *Ouvert et innocent.* We talked about Laurent. How he could be a pain but we should have helped him more. His murder went unsolved for many years. I don't exactly know when DNA testing got more sophisticated, but they caught his killer because of DNA in 1991. Turns out that Laurent had some cash and this guy wanted it, they fought and that's what happened. For money. The amount was ridiculous. There is a true crime book on the case called *La ruelle* and we're all in it including the rumours. The killer was in the system, in jail already and he confessed to killing Laurent. The journalist André Cyr pieced it together, the timeline of Laurent going to a bar on lower St-Laurent near Old Montréal with money to score. And the guy basically was outside and made a snap decision to follow Laurent and roll him for whatever he had. Crime of opportunity. It ended the way we know. Laurent was found just inside an alley a day or two later. There is even a photo of Carl-Yves, me and Laurent taken at VidPop in the book. At this very table.

I wanted to surprise everybody with business cards so I ordered a small amount from this print place. Carl hated them right away. He thought it made us look like some regular business organization.

CARL-YVES DUBÉ We all wanted to honour his memory. So we came up with the idea of having a kind of wake at Vidéo Populaire. We held it a week after his funeral. It was not good. Some of our friends came, some Vidéo Populaire members and board and some of Laurent's friends who thought we were guilty of something, not all of them, but a few were on that track. They thought we were being insincere, taking advantage, doing some fake mourning. One guy accused me or us of stealing some of Laurent's notebooks that we were going to publish as our own or use his words in a video or something like that. I don't remember how that night ended. I like to think I didn't hit anybody.

ANDRÉ CYR Talk about a cold case. The police had nothing. They kind of hit on Vidéo Populaire because there were links between them and Laurent. You can just imagine these detectives show up and see what they think are a bunch of hippies doing god knows what. It was a culture clash, pure and simple. No evidence, just a business card. The officers kept asking 'what do you do here, what is it you do?' When I was writing *La ruelle*, I went to the new office of Vidéo Populaire to meet with Terry and Lydia, re-inteview them and get permissions for photographs. I tried very hard to find Carl-Yves. And I did find him, but he refused to talk on the subject. For Maurice, there was no way. I kind of thought Terry and Lydia were acting like *chiens de garde*, but I remembered Maurice was not very

29

forthcoming so I dropped it. It was more for background anyhow.

MAURICE AUBERT We were just getting started. Everything was new. I already saw Laurent with us, in the future. I was mortified that people could think bad things like that about Carl and me. Carl told me we would get through it together. Our friends knew we were not involved in any way. Carl pulled me along with him. We all wanted to keep going. But I couldn't stop thinking about Laurent and how he was stopped from keeping going. I saw the photograph from the crime scene. The police showed it to us. They never should have done that. It was the worst thing they could have done. I've never been able to get it out of my head. It still shows up, too, it's like someone just shoves the image in front of my eyes. In that photo you could just make out a notebook. It was found next to him. Laurent had dozens of notebooks. All the same kind that were found in his apartment. Laurent was a chaos guy but those notebooks were all numbered.

LYDIA CARTWRIGHT Some of my sadness wasn't straightforward. I was sad for Laurent and his family and friends, that part was clear. I was sad for me, but I didn't know why. Maybe I still don't; probably feeling sorry for myself. I was sad because VidPop was precarious, it depended on people who were fragile, really, and we didn't even know it, not yet. Laurent had been part of it even if only for a short time. Laurent was being referred to as 'troubled' and such and we kept thinking in twenty years is that all that people will be able to say about him? 'Troubled poet Laurent Simard.' Turns out no. Guys like Serge Masson and Michael are more present in the official history but aren't necessarily deserving.

CARL-YVES DUBÉ I knew we had nothing to do with his death, but we all had to live with the idea that we might have been able to change things. This or that action could have made a difference. A fraction of a second. I wonder sometimes if his death didn't radicalize me more. I thought we were running out of time.

I fucking hate *Allô police*. But I have two issues of it at home in a box, the one from 1975 and the one where it was announced that the case was closed.

Maurice and I used to do something together once a year or so as a memorial. We would watch the images Maurice took of Laurent performing *Karawane*. Just us. No one else saw those images. I used to think, good, these are private in a way. I've been wondering if Maurice still has those images. I've been wondering if he incorporated them in one of his videos.

LYDIA CARTWRIGHT   It was daunting. All of it. The aftermath of his death. And how we were all trying to move forward and we didn't even know what that meant, moving forward. There was a certain amount of shunning. Some people believed we, or Carl and Maurice, were guilty of something.

One thing that people won't know is that Maurice had one of Laurent's notebooks. It was a gift. Maurice sent the notebook to Laurent's best friend, anonymously. The friend, I know his first name is Bernard, but I'm not getting his family name...anyhow, Bernard came to the wake, kept his distance but was not aggressive. He tried to calm other people down about the whole murder rap. Maurice asked Carl to help him write a note. They cut letters out of the newspaper, like for a ransom note. 'Laurent is a brilliant poet and writer. Please do everything you can to get his work published.' It was very difficult for Maurice to part with the notebook.

MYLÈNE BOISJOLI One of the last things I remember when Carl and I were still together was trying to be there for him during that whole time.

That wake at Vidéo Populaire was so bizarre. There was a strange mix of people, some of Laurent's family, some of his friends, those of us associated with Vidéo Populaire in some way. It was tense. Carl-Yves was playing some of Laurent's favourite videos on a monitor, and one of the relatives kept asking why the TV was on, it was disrespectul, turn the TV off.

ANDRÉ CYR Much later on, I thought it would be interesting to write about that era. My idea was to look at three different organizations and their approach to community activism. I thought back to the time I spent at Vidéo Populaire and there was something interesting. I didn't know anything about video but between Carl-Yves and Lydia I felt like I got a good introductory course. That wake was surreal. People think I exaggerated it for my book, but I didn't.

PIERRE NADEAU After Laurent, I started going to Vidéo Populaire regularly, in earnest. There was a change in Maurice. He had these interests, like, he knew everything there was to know about the Titanic. Jack the Ripper. He could tell you dates and names of the women and the list of suspects. Yma Sumac. Francis Picabia. He never talked much, but if you wanted him to, you started the conversation with one of those topics. If you sat down and talked to Maurice, you had to be prepared for any response. I would ask him what he was working on and he would talk about Anita O'Day's interpretation of 'That Old Feeling.' I learned a lot because our talks were so all over the place. Anyhow, it was then that I noticed more what people would call his eccentricities. After Laurent.

ROSEMARY DRUMMOND I was an acquaintance of Lydia's. I used to go by 'Rainbo.' Lydia never called me 'Rainbo' because she would just start giggling and couldn't stop. Ahead of her time, I guess. I found out years later that Sissy Spacek had cut a record under the pseudonym 'Rainbo', so my nickname wasn't even original. By the end of the seventies, I was Rosemary again, though quite a few people would remember me as 'Rainbo.'

I warned Lydia not to throw in with those three guys, because I thought she would just get used. I used to think I could read people, see their auras. I pegged Carl-Yves as trouble. I saw Maurice as sad. For me, Terry was a bit paternalistic, controlling. I told Lydia all of this and she's like 'I can handle them.' There was some fucked up aura there, but it wasn't all bad. Some of it was great.

Laurent had died and people were being weird about VidPop as if they were some kind of band of commie video assassins. I actually threw in with them because they were getting a bad rap. I just think we were too radical politically. You only had to spend a few minutes with Maurice to know he was incapable of violence. Carl-Yves, okay, much more likely, but here's the thing about him, he was a serious hothead, with a moral code like I've rarely seen.

ROSAIRE LACHANCE Back in those days, I wanted to break into radio or TV. Expressing an ambition like that in that crowd was to hear things like 'vendu.' I didn't know how you got experience to work in TV, so I was looking around. I knew Maurice from school. We went to the same high school. When he formed Vidéo Populaire with the others, I thought maybe they could use some on-camera interviewers. I went out with that one guy Carl-Yves and Maurice to shoot some vox populi, people on the street segments. 'What are your feelings about the October crisis?' was one question. We were five years on from 1970 but it was still a huge part of how we felt. 'What do you think the government could do to help the poor?' I think maybe I did this a few times with them. It didn't lead anywhere for me. I went back to see the final edit. I asked Carl-Yves if I could have a copy to use for job interviews to help break me into broadcasting. He said no. And then he lectured me. Something about the videos being shown in a specific context. And that the video belonged to the collective or organization. And that the work was not to further my own career. I got the point, okay, okay, but he was such an asshole about it. I ended up doing community radio and then later on got a job as a radio announcer, then I had some of my own shows.

DANIELLE AUBERT   Our parents were both only children. We don't have cousins and aunts and uncles. It's just Maurice and I who remember our childhood. He has half our family photos and I have the other half. We see each other each Sunday for lunch or dinner except when I'm out of town.

I was eighteen and still living at home when VidPop happened. Maurice would come for dinner and tell me about these people and these stories and I was fascinated, although I didn't understand really at all. It's funny, because everyone always notices how quiet Maurice is but he's always told me stories and jokes to make me laugh.

LYDIA CARTWRIGHT   I was going to school and working as a waitress. I even took babysitting jobs to earn extra and pay my share of the camera and contribute to the rent.

We moved a few times. Terry's apartment was first, that tiny room. It was okay for meetings but we had to get something bigger for the equipment. Then we rented our first space on St-Laurent and Prince-Arthur. That was 1975-1981. Then up the street to Rachel. That was 1981-1989. Where else? 1989, we went to Rivard and Marie-Anne. Then in 1997 we found what is the current location on Berri. We were pretty lucky in a sense, being a non-profit group that didn't have to move too often.

I remember the feeling of that first space. I'd held a lot of jobs since I was fifteen, mostly dead-end ones and mostly as a waitress. Now it was like part of that place belonged to me, or the opposite. I wasn't showing up for a paycheque. There was no paycheque anyhow. It was the feeling.

MAURICE AUBERT   I was there during the St-Laurent period. After Terry's place, we were on the Main for a while. The soundtrack of 1974-1975 was...I liked *Harmonium* and so did the other three. We didn't all agree on *Beau Dommage*. I was surprised that Carl-Yves got into *Heart Like a Wheel* by Linda Ronstadt. Her voice won him over.

I'm sure I've always done regular things. You pretty much have to, things like sleeping and eating, breathing, walking, all that. I don't sleep very well for long stretches, so I kind of have little naps throughout the day. There are lots of foods I can eat, but there are certain things I really love.

At Vidéo Populaire, I went through a serious popcorn sandwich period. Loved them, wouldn't eat much else. Don't have them anymore. Too gritty. Right now I eat avocados, ramen, bananas, sardines from a can, mayonnaise, Fanta, almonds, oranges, nectarines. Maybe it looks restrictive. I think there are probably worse diets than mine.

I just wanted to make videos and play around with editing. I loved those first machines. As soon as better ones came along, everybody was like 'these are better, these are faster, these do more.' I liked the old ones. They are in good working order. I maintain them.

ROSEMARY DRUMMOND I'd been doing all kinds of things, travelling across the States, living on communes, getting fucked up. Montréal was supposed to be short-term but I had to earn some bread to leave again. I hung out with Lydia a bit. We knew each other from Concordia and also theatre stuff. I kept telling her to do the same thing, the video collective but with three other women. She got it, but she was a woman of her word and was loyal. Carl-Yves made a stupid joke. He Francisized everything so Rainbo became Arc-en-ciel only he took the 'el' away because I took the 'double u' away from Rainbo. I became Arc-en-cie. So I show up in the credits for one of his videos as R. Cancy. Ha, ha. With guys like that around it was a relief to be Rosemary again.

I left after that whole Laurent mess and forgot all about the place until maybe a year or so later when I came back to Montréal. Still there. Lydia still with the guys. And it was working. So I conceded the point and got more involved. I'm going to say it was 1977.

MICHAEL STIRKIN   It lasted quite long that video thing with Lydia I guess. I saw her in the paper a few times talking about what they were up to. She was vaguely famous. The last time I saw her I think I walked her over to a meeting or something and she didn't want me to come in. I thought she was embarrassed to be seen with me because I was so unlike all those guys she was hanging with. She said no, but I didn't believe her and said so and then she just said we should think about ending it because we were going in different directions. It was very quick, what she did, just sort of dumped me on the sidewalk and went up to her revolutionary buddies or whatever. I couldn't believe she chose those losers.

DANIELLE AUBERT   We lived in Outremont in a very nice house. Maurice would entertain our mother and me by telling us about some of the people he was meeting and some of the situations that arose at VidPop. I really wanted him to invite me to visit him there. I was so curious, but shy to ask. Finally he did and I went. It was the opposite of every place I knew in my life at that point. I was going to a private school, attending a nice church, Catholic of course, and hanging out in houses that looked just like ours. I went to Vidéo Populaire and saw a sparse office with strange furniture and multicoloured walls and these people that looked like people I was supposed to avoid. The floor was concrete and it was painted different colours, too. Maurice had long hair and wore jeans, but he was always well-groomed, well-dressed in his own way. My first impression of Carl-Yves was that he was kind of a wild man. His hair was longer than mine and he had a full beard and moustache. He said 'Salut' instead of saying something more formal. Terrence was very polite, engaged me in conversation. I was fascinated by Lydia because I had never met a woman like her before. I kept trying to figure out if maybe she was with Carl-Yves or Terry, stupid girl that I was. The whole place kind of intimidated me.

TERRENCE O'MEARA It was almost like we gathered around the camera. I have an image in my head and it might not be true but that we put the camera case on the table and all of us stared at it then opened it like some treasure chest. I mean, we weren't the first with utopic ideas to congregate around a camera but it felt so new.

Lost images. We have some of those at VidPop, never migrated to a current format. I dropped the ball. It took me a long time to understand that I was the only one who was paying attention after a certain point. I remembered the images as so vibrant and immediate. I thought they would last. When video formats started changing and changing, going from huge to small, it was too late for some of them. Now I'm very careful. Everything gets migrated to a current format. The lost images aren't really lost. They are on reels and these are stacked in a locker. I know there are places and people out there who can transfer them for me, but I can't let them out of my sight. I'm afraid they will disappear forever. If I can see the reels, look at the old formats, I still feel like I can call up those images. Someday I'm going to give someone I trust the key to VidPop and the one to the locker and say 'have them transferred.'

When we first started, we didn't have desks or anything like that. We had a big table, huge, that's where we sat, but no one had an individual workspace. We got in the habit of keeping our personal stuff in these banker's boxes that I bought. Predictably, I hid the name 'Banker's Box' from Carl by blacking it out, because that would have been enough to set him off. When Carl left and didn't come back, his box just sat under the table. I didn't touch the box for a long time. We decided to move the table one day. The box was there, marked Carl-Yves. I finally got up the courage to look in it. There was a sheet with Carl's writing on it, looked like ideas for a video. And there was a tape. $3/4$", unlabelled. That's all. I mailed the sheet to Carl at the address we had for him, but the letter came back, return to sender. After the letter came back, I took the tape and I handed it to Maurice. That was a mistake. He almost dropped it when he heard it had been in Carl's box. He shoved it back at me and told me not to keep it at VidPop, to send it on to Carl right away. I told him the address we had for Carl was not good anymore. At first I didn't think he had registered what I'd said. Maurice followed me back to the box and he ordered me to put the tape and sheet back in. This is Maurice, he never ordered anybody to do anything. He wanted the box taped shut. Then he wanted me to leave with the box, take it home, just get it out of there. He watched me go down the hall and out the door. I asked him if there was something on that tape that was disturbing but he would never answer. He just said it couldn't be there, at VidPop.

I still have the box.

DAN BRISEBOIS I thought it was exciting for them. My friend was Terry. I didn't know the others at all at first. Terry and I met on a few construction jobs. We hit it off because we were the only two on this job site who brought books to read on lunch break. I got the impression that a few of their friends kind of followed them as they were starting VidPop. I helped build a few shelves, paint the office. Terry wanted me to stay on, be a member, but I had zero interest in politics and didn't know anything about video. He wanted to do something a bit more with his life. He kind of stuck with construction jobs for a time but then he stopped for VidPop.

LYDIA CARTWRIGHT You know what really worked back then? The mix of us. Carl was more flinty and that really anchored Maurice. He also kind of propelled Terry and me. Terry had a slight tendency to get lost in the sheer amount of things that needed doing and Carl was a good counterbalance for all of us. I really focused on staying with our plan since I was always losing interest in things and moving on. To my surprise, VidPop and those guys held my attention. I was in it and that was just so...restful after years of jumping from thing to thing.

Back at the beginning, Terry would arrive sometimes with a hard hat from working construction. Carl would be coming from one of his grocery store jobs. I was coming from waitressing. Maurice had a job back then, too. He worked at a library part-time. He would often be at VidPop kind of waiting for us with fresh coffee. I couldn't wait to get there. I couldn't wait to see them.

CARL-YVES DUBÉ The first real office was huge. We didn't have much. We each took things from our own apartments and contributed them to the cause. I think I had two chairs to my name and I brought one to Vidéo Populaire. Lamps, tables, stuff like that, all mismatched. Maurice brought a door from his place, he walked it over and we put it on two sawhorses. Instant table. I bet some of that stuff is still there. Lydia contributed a rug that her grandmother had given her. She hated it but couldn't throw it out for sentimental reasons. I wonder sometimes if it is very Ikea chic at the Vidéo Populaire office now. We also never said 'office.' We used 'space.' Terrence brought in his portable record player. It was supposed to be temporary but it stayed for as long as I was there.

Maurice told me he thought there was a ghost. I didn't know what to say, I mean, a ghost? He said he could feel and see things. I never saw or felt anything. But I guess I wouldn't. It was rare for anyone to be there alone. We were almost always together in the first few years so I told him that it would be okay because of that. Rainbo was around then and she would look and look at Maurice. It kind of freaked him out.

I always really loved that Maurice stuck to his guns about the Lumière screening story. I do think he really believed that shit. Weren't there all these people claiming they had been at that café in Paris? Impossible because the café only had room for so many people...I goaded him into trying to convince Terry that another of his relatives was in a Meliès movie to see if that would catch on, too. Maurice was upset with me for teasing him. The look in his eyes.

I was getting to know him. I began to understand that there were things he would say...well, he wasn't joking or trying to convince you of something.

SERGE MASSON I really didn't get involved at all beyond a certain point. When they were looking for a space and they found one I was impressed because they were doing it. I thought it was all talk. I was curious so I went there once or twice. How long would the two Anglophone new-age granolas, Lydia and Terry, last with Carl-Yves, who had some kind of great liberator complex? Maurice I met there and I couldn't figure him out at all, how he fit with the others. He was quiet, kind of motionless while the others were constantly moving.

Carl invited me to those early meetings. They were looking for board members. I think he thought I was his protégé. That he was moulding me. I didn't know anything about anything. I admit it. He was pretty charismatic. I disappointed him. I know that because he wrote me a postcard telling me I betrayed the cause.

MAURICE AUBERT I don't know if it's one ghost that follows me around or what. Rainbo saw it, too, once. I've always had this. I can tell you that both offices I was in were haunted. Telling Carl was good because he was the most factual guy, like he had his two feet in reality every minute of every day. I would tell him things and immediately in his eyes I would read 'impossible, does not compute.'

I wonder if the ghost didn't come with the camera? Because when we brought it home to VidPop I was really excited but something more, too. Something else, but I don't know how to put it in words.

ROSEMARY DRUMMOND I think I might have agreed with Moe about the ghost business just to support him, because it turns out I wasn't a gifted clairvoyant at all but I could see this guy was struggling. I did think I was plugged into something back then, some psychic crap.

Oh shit. I may have done a kind of ritual for Moe...at VidPop. To ask the ghost to leave. Knowing me, it would have been a combo of feminist slogans and stuff, like burning sage. I believed it then. Open all the windows and doors and kind of sweep the place. Lydia asked me 'what the difference was between that and spring cleaning.' Oh she saw right through me. Which I didn't like at the time.

CARL-YVES DUBÉ The best memory for me was when we finally had the camera and we were trying to decide what to shoot first. I thought it was important that we begin with something we really wanted to capture, like we were introducing this camera to its job, what it would be doing for the next years. I didn't even want to do tests or anything like that. Our first shot had to be something we would absolutely use in a production. Not my normal logic, I guess, but I felt really strongly about that. I convinced everyone, let's go outside, let's go on the street, let's see what happens.

TERRENCE O'MEARA Carl was shouting 'venez-vous-en' from the door, waving us out. It was contagious. I was kind of in awe of the camera. I was afraid I wouldn't measure up. Maurice and Carl were in awe but in a different way. They couldn't wait to get started. I had the manual out and was reading aloud. No one was listening.

MAURICE AUBERT Carl hogged the camera. I started going in very early to get a chance to try it out. Terry and Lydia couldn't get near it and we had a talk with Carl saying the camera belonged to all of us and we were supposed to be collaborating on a video. It was actually pretty funny. He apologized. He was just so excited. He was mooning over it.

LYDIA CARTWRIGHT That camera was heavy. Portable but heavy. I still think about that when I use cameras today. That heft. Maurice and Carl were kind of adorable around it. Now thirty some years on, more, I wonder if that wasn't the first little difference between us, the first sign of an infinitesimal split. Those two were crazy about that camera and shooting and editing. Terry and I hung back a little, were a bit afraid, intimidated.

CARL-YVES DUBÉ The discussions began. What were we going to say? How to begin? I was of two minds about a script. We didn't know how to write one. I also thought that it could be too limiting, fascist even, to have a script. But for our first video it would be good to have some structure. So Terry got these big sheets of paper that we taped to the wall and we wrote down ideas. We were there a lot, talking and discussing. When we weren't at our shitty jobs, we were there. I would describe *Four More Years* by TVTV to them because I loved it and I wanted our work to be something like that. That was the template for me. It wasn't just about the content; it had to be about how we made it, the decisions we took as we shot and edited.

MAURICE AUBERT It wasn't easy to see videos then, not like now. Now people hand you a DVD. Or they send you a link. Carl would describe these whole parts of videos to us. He would put his whole body into it. I loved watching his versions of videos. I really liked *Ant Farm's Dirty Dishes* by Ant Farm, which we managed to see...how I don't remember. Ant Farm taped what they were doing, kind of integrating the Portapak into their days, their daily activities. I really loved Jean-Pierre Boyer's work. So beautiful. He built his own machine, the Boyétizeur. I felt like I wanted to go that way, towards abstraction and more experimental work, but I put it off, because Carl had me convinced about...the importance of the real. The new documentary.

I came up with the idea of taping that whole thing we did where we sat in the office discussing and writing things down on the walls. In one shot, you can make out big words on paper like 'travail,' 'societé' and 'outils.' The text underneath those words was too small to show up. I shot

Terry and Carl and Lydia each taking turns writing on the paper.

TERRENCE O'MEARA Maurice wrestled the camera away from Carl for part of that process. I think we spent hours writing and talking. I have no idea how many hours we taped of that. What ended up in the video is minimal but that idea was good, it kind of anchored us, because it was self-reflexive and we were all into that from different movies. Maurice actually talked about the cartoon "Duck Amuck" where Daffy Duck realizes he is in a cartoon. The background and Daffy's clothes keep changing. You even see the giant pencil the animator is using. Cue the explosion from Carl! He couldn't believe that Daffy Duck was being mentioned as we were making history. I think he spent the next hour lecturing us and a lot of it is on tape about Michel Brault and Jean Rouch and Chris Marker and TVTV and how they had to be our models, not some duck. Poor Maurice.

CARL-YVES DUBÉ When we were together in those first years we worked so well and got so much done. We kind of coalesced. That first video we made — all four of us — is called *Vidéo Populaire* and is like a tour of our space and our politics and how to make video in 1974-1975 according to us. It shows the office in detail. It shows the view from our windows. It shows those sheets of paper with the text on them. That dumb door/table. Maurice was a natural. He picked up the camera and knew it. It knew him. I was amazed at how good he was. A little jealous, too. I had to practice.

You know what I like? I can't really remember who shot what for those early videos. It could have been any of us four and also Antonio (Dutto) and Pierre (Nadeau).

It's stupid, ridiculous, but that's how I most see myself, like I was back then. I used to have a recurring dream where I turn a corner in a corridor and there is a mirror.

I look and my reflection is young Carl from around that time. I haven't been that or looked like that for forty years... it's the version of me that stays most, I guess.

ISABELLE MERCIER-LALONDE I don't remember how I heard about them. Or when. They were around. I went to a lot of *manifs* back then and I suppose they did, too, with their camera. Carl-Yves knew one of the guys I worked with. There was a rumour that this group was going to do TV shows, but about things that were important.

LYDIA CARTWRIGHT I laughed a lot with those guys. Some of the clashes were not that funny at the time but in retrospect...About that first camera. Terry and I were holding ourselves back. We would actually leave the office and talk about our apprehensions. Terry said we should start treating the camera like the wizard in *The Wizard of Oz* when he's discovered behind the curtain and he keeps saying 'I am the great and powerful Oz.' Dedramatizing the camera. We would go into the hall around the corner to the back stairs and laugh at ourselves. I'm going to say we did not share our fears with the other two. It worked because I learned and Terry did, too.

MAURICE AUBERT I watch *Vidéo Populaire* every once in a while. It is like having my friends back.

MICHAEL STIRKIN I just couldn't understand what they were going to do with themselves. I mean, they weren't going to be cameramen for the news or anything like that. They had zero experience. They weren't serious film-makers. Hollywood wasn't calling. I couldn't see it leading to anything career-wise. None of them was a director. I couldn't imagine that anyone would want to see what they were making, because it was so different and kind of hostile and the images were fuzzy, just bad. They were always correcting me — 'we're not making films, we're making videos.' Whatever.

TERRENCE O'MEARA We weren't the only people who were excited. It was everywhere then, that feeling, the zeitgeist. I feel like I didn't sleep for five years. We were go, go, go. We believed in an independent Québec, socialism, peace, equality for all and we thought that video would be one of the tools to help get us there. *Un chausson avec ça?*

ANTONIO DUTTO I became friends with Carl when he was in New York. We met at an event, a happening. I think 1973. Videos were presented but I can't tell you which ones. I didn't know much but I knew a few people who were in that scene. I'm embarrassed to say that I didn't understand that there was a whole French culture just above New York State. I was from Pittsburgh, you'd think I'd have known, it wasn't that far from the border. I thought he was from France because of his accent. Oh man, you can imagine how that went over. He sat me down and explained it all to me, the language thing, the oppression, his feelings about a separate country. I was blown away. I told him about my brother, Giuseppe, Joe, who was a few years older than me and had been in Vietnam and came back completely fucked up. Joe joined the anti-war movement when he came back home in late '71. I had a Super 8 camera and was always shooting stuff. I took images of Joe getting home in his uniform with his eyes all hard and small and weird. Carl and I were both in our early twenties and both not sure what we wanted to do and we hit it off because we liked what we saw there that night. And because we just blurted these personal things out and we weren't really like that, either of us. We didn't spill our guts to strangers.

Carl called me up and told me about the VidPop project. I finally went up to Montréal to visit him and see for myself in the first year they were established. Man, that was something to see. That was inspiring. I felt more and more like I had to do something with my brother and take a look at his experiences in the war and his activism after he came back.

PIERRE NADEAU I think I may have been among the first gang of members. I don't think that there were even hours of operation. It was just open, it seemed, all the time and people were always there. I was friends with a friend of Carl-Yves's girlfriend, Mylène. Small world. My friend invited me to the *pendaison de crémaillère*, the housewarming, if you can say that for a video centre. Oh, funny story, I barely spoke English then and I said to some anglo woman 'come, we are going to hang the creamer' because *pendre* is hang and *crémaillère* is the creamer, but it makes no sense. I was always making mistakes like that.

For me, it was a way of belonging. All the other stuff I tried I was just miserable at. The usual things that you were supposed to love, like hockey. At Vidéo Populaire I could actually say to other guys that I found Hockey Night in Canada boring and depressing. The theme song would make me anxious.

MAURICE AUBERT I went to VidPop every day for as long as I was part of it. Except for one day only because of a massive winter storm. The sidewalks were full of snow with tiny corridors where people tramped it down. My cat hadn't come back. I was worried. We don't get storms like that as often anymore. Even though none of us went to the space, we called each other and talked on the phone. I didn't like that day. We all had those black rotary phones. I would picture them sitting or standing when we talked on the phone. I still have mine. I should ask Terry and Lydia what their phones are like now so I can picture them when we talk.

I felt trapped at home. The worst is November. It gets dark early. And you have four months to go.

Our first office space was home. I never wanted to leave. When Carl left, the others were talking about a new start in a new space. I didn't want to. I used to think Carl would come back but he would only do that if we stayed put. We didn't and he stayed away. I tried the second space. I gave it four years. The ghost came with us. Or another one was already there.

DAN BRISEBOIS Every once in a while, I would stop in and see Terry. I liked my regular jobs in construction. A regular schedule. Those things worked for me. My impression of the place was that you went if you needed to find yourself. A lot of people did find something. And others like me went because they knew someone. Like I said, I went sporadically and I would notice there seemed to be more and more people there each time I dropped in. Not crowds or anything but it was four of them then more then the last time I went it was some kind of event so there were lots. I built some shelves, that was my contribution. I helped Maurice by building these special stands for a machine he was working on. I drifted away because I started working a lot in construction. I wasn't like them, the place was not my life.

LYDIA CARTWRIGHT We were there. We were in it and couldn't imagine anything else. I refuse to be condescending about us because we held beliefs that fell out of fashion.

Antonio visited because he was a friend of Carl's. He shot some of the footage that is in *Vidéo Populaire*. Great guy. Because of Antonio, we know that Carl is still around. He is very discreet, but he lets us know that Carl is doing okay.

We introduced Antonio to just about everything we had to offer: video, Marxism, good coffee, Québec politics and probably much more besides, including some of our huge disagreements. He became our first member, our first 'membre-travailleur.' Of course, he didn't speak a word of French apart from 'bonjour' and 'merci' at first. That was okay with Carl because he was American. We introduced him to Molson Ex beer, which was what we drank until Carl and Moe came to the conclusion that we shouldn't be supporting a company that they saw as colonizers. We switched to another brand. I sometimes wonder what micro-brew beer we would favour now.

CARL-YVES DUBÉ   I keep in touch with Antonio. His brother Joe, Giuseppe, passed away a few years ago from cancer and I went down for the funeral. I made sure the others weren't going. I stayed with Antonio and his wife, Claudia. We drank to Joe, and Antonio wanted to talk about the old days. He asked me why I couldn't be part of Vidéo Populaire again or something like that. Him and Giuseppe had always hung out together over the years but Antonio was worried he hadn't been there for him somehow. He didn't want me to feel the same way about Vidéo Populaire.

MAURICE AUBERT   It was good to see us through someone else's eyes, Antonio's. I loved the way he looked at us. He kept saying he was 'blown away.' Not everyone made it into our group at first but he was one of us. The other guy I really liked was Pierre (Nadeau). He had a kind of shape just over his left shoulder that was a good colour. It made me feel good to look at it. Rosemary I didn't dislike but I think she thought I was up to something at first, because she would look at me and look at me. Dan you didn't have to feel obliged to chat with at all. He would show up sometimes and hang out. He built some cool stuff. I could tell he liked us but that he wouldn't stay. It was kind of written all over him. I asked if I could tape him doing some of the work, the shelves and the stands for my Moechines. He said okay and so Dan is in a few of my videos. Laurent's eyes, of course. And his voice.

TERRENCE O'MEARA   After we had bought the camera and worked on our first production, we started discussing what we all felt might be the next step. The idea was to open it up a bit, have an active membership. I say things and I want to rephrase right away. I mean I say things and it sounds like it was easy but it wasn't. Nothing was, really. We had board members and the four of us, that's ten or eleven people total all trying to figure out this membership thing. Who could be a member? We were a political entity. Would we accept anyone?

48

CARL-YVES DUBÉ *Membres-travailleurs* status was reserved for the four of us and Antonio as an honorary...status I guess. Maybe Nadeau as well. Rosemary, possibly. Laurent was gone. He would have been one. But then later on when there were other employees, they were also *membres-travailleurs* too. *Membres-producteurs* was for videomakers who were committed to the Vidéo Populaire mandate. *Membres-associés* was for people who wanted to use our equipment, but not just for any project. We had to approve it.

More than once we refused a project. One guy came to us wanting to be a *membre-associé* and we said okay tell us what you are going to make. His idea was to make a documentary about homeless people. He had no real idea, he just thought it was interesting. He didn't know any homeless people, wasn't in contact, hadn't built relationships, sans-dessin. I think he even said that he would buy them a steamé and fries. Just show up and start capturing them? No way. That's exactly the kind of method we were criticizing. I remember that well, because once a year or so where I teach a student will come up with that same idea, about showing homeless people. And I say no way.

LYDIA CARTWRIGHT These two guys showed up once to sign up as membres-associés and talk about a video idea they had. Our policy was to always have two of us to screen video proposals. So they begin talking and basically they are espousing some anti-woman ideas, how feminism was a scourge, how men were getting soft. At one point I thought it might have been a joke, someone rattling our cage because we had a reputation for political correctness even before the term existed. I just lost it. Carl-Yves lost it on them even worse than I did. He was spectacular and I will love him for that until the day I die.

TERRENCE O'MEARA The idea was not to impose our own views but to encourage a new kind of production. There were a lot of rejections, especially in the first years. Us four, we had to go through the same process to get our own projects accepted. Was your project bourgeois? Was your project innovative in both form and content? What was your intent?

CÉCILE GRONDIN   That whole process of defining membership took quite a long time. At other places, video or film centres, you didn't have to adhere to political ideas to gain access. If Carl-Yves had had his way, the membership policy would have been a huge document.

ANTONIO DUTTO   Definitely different from what I knew about groups in the US, political but not in the same way. Vidéo Populaire had a code. It wasn't freewheeling like you come in off the street and pitch your idea and anything goes. But when I was there I did see some of that, the four of them enjoying themselves, serious but fun, too. And you see that in those early collaborations like *Vidéo Populaire*.

MAURICE AUBERT   Carl really wanted to show videos at VidPop, have screenings. We would all sit together and watch tapes. At first, it seems like it was just us four. Then Pierre. Then Rosemary. Then I turned around in my chair and there were others. Quite a few.

DANIELLE AUBERT   I did not go there often. I saw my brother often, though. He always had time for me, which was very sweet because I was the opposite of him at that time, I was a bit of a snooty stuck-up girl. I probably thought the VidPop thing was dingy, shoddy, just because it wasn't standard. He brought me to see some videos. I had no idea what I was looking at. Later, he invited me over to show me what he was working on. He explained some of his ideas to me. I'm not sure I understood at all but it dawned on me that Maurice saw me as someone who could understand.

CARL-YVES DUBÉ   There used to be this debate about whether videos should only be shown on monitors, or projected. I was only for monitors because they were for me the natural way to present video. The others thought so, too. Most video artists felt the same way. We agreed that video *belonged* to monitors. Well, projectors and screens won in the long run obviously. That's almost all you see in museums and galleries now, videos pretending to be films.

I practically invented a whole other debate all by myself as I like to do. I know my reputation. I liked black and white for video. Colour was available, of course, but I wanted Vidéo Populaire to stay away from it. Maybe because some of my favourite tapes were in black and white. The monitor thing most people agreed on but the black and white thing just got me looks. Maurice was really liking the possibilities of colour. He used my own method on me by feeding me lists of good work shot in colour. On one list, he put down all these films I hated — as a joke — like musicals. Anybody who sees Maurice just one way is missing most of him.

TERRENCE O'MEARA Those video presentations were held once a month and they became very popular. We picked a day, Wednesday, and we stuck with it for a long, long time. Like decades. We only had room for about forty people but sometimes more than that would show up. We had two monitors we used and would set them up to make two viewing areas. Video festivals used to privilege presentation on monitors. That really dates us now. So does saying 'tape,' I imagine. Because often there is no tape.

LYDIA CARTWRIGHT   I sometimes knocked Carl for being too rigid with all the political stuff. I mean, I was in it, too, just as Marxist as he was, although I'm sure he would disagree. There had to be some leeway. We had to be flexible, I thought, or we would become this one thing like painting ourselves into the proverbial corner. But the video presentations were great even though they were tinged with our politics. I thought the events were a way of reaching out to other people who might not be on board politically but would like this newish medium.

DR. TIMOTHY PETERSON That's a photo of me and the four of them taken in 1977. People always ask me about that photograph, what I was doing with all those hippie types, me in my scrubs, short hair, clean shaven.

My first office was in the same building as Vidéo Populaire. We were both on the first floor. I noticed that there were always people coming in and out of their office and I had no idea what they did there. They were certainly doing better business than me. I was curious so I went over. I was so square I thought offices were for dentists and doctors and chartered accountants. They weren't doing business at all. Not in the sense that I understood it. I'd been on a mission to get out of school and set up my practice. I did that and then I looked around and saw all the other great things I had ignored for years. My mother had been an art lover. I guess I became one, too.

I introduced myself to Terrence and Lydia and Carl-Yves. I asked what they did. And they patiently told me. I would leave my office late and see people milling around outside the VidPop door and I would go over. I saw videos there. My world wasn't changed or anything but I certainly loved a lot of it.

CARL-YVES DUBÉ Maurice did something once that just sent me over the edge. 1978 maybe. At one of our parties. Or I should say happenings. He was doing his signal process stuff in the front, a kind of performance, only he started doing it on some of my images! I hated that shit and he knew it. I was all for images that were realistic and there he goes making my images curl up into themselves and explode apart and stuff like that. Like everyone else, I guess I was watching and I was pretty amazed by what I was seeing until I realized he was fucking with some of the striking workers I'd been interviewing. I threw myself at him. Probably somebody separated us before it degenerated but I don't remember. If anyone else had done that...

ROSEMARY DRUMMOND   Carl-Yves had a reputation for being one mean motherfucker. True-ish but certainly not all the time. I was not always the biggest fan of Carl's, but I kind of got something new from him that time. Maurice was not completely innocent, he knew how Carl didn't like the artsy stuff. So I kind of felt we learned two things after that event: Carl was a purist and Maurice could be a little shit disturber. Carl was on a mission.

The parties we used to have were free-form, videos being shown on monitors, bands. You could leave, have a nap, come back and it would still be going on.

PIERRE NADEAU   I was having a nice time looking at those images Maurice was manipulating and thinking 'wow.' I think I knew something was off but I didn't grasp it. That's a legend, another one...the idea that the events of that night put a wedge between Carl-Yves and Maurice. I don't think that's true. They were okay after that, still always with each other working on stuff.

MAURICE AUBERT   I thought I could show Carl that our ideas about video were the same.

TERRENCE O'MEARA   Pierre and I saved Maurice from having the shit kicked out of him by Carl.

MYLÈNE BOISJOLI   I was there. Carl-Yves and I had found each other again. We did that, too, breaking up and getting back together. I think that was our last hurrah.

I was laughing because I thought Carl-Yves was joking about how angry he was, making a big thing of it to be funny. No. Maurice did not see that coming. I did not see that coming. Carl-Yves always had lots of energy, ideas and drive. You could feel the electricity coming off of him, but I had never seen him like that.

DR. TIMOTHY PETERSON   I think some people misremember that an ambulance was called. It wasn't, at least not to my recollection. I think people got confused because I was there in my scrubs. I used to wander over to VidPop after I finished work. Carl used to get a kick out of it, me showing up dressed like that.

DAVID SUMMERVILLE No, no, no, I didn't think they were too much, those VidPop people. I mean I was one of those VidPop people, too. The four of them is what I mean to say. Maurice was way out there. They got along great when I was around. It was exciting. You would go there and hey, watch out for Carl-Yves and what's Maurice up to? He's editing of course. And if you wanted to relax from those two there was Terry and Lydia. I went around there because I thought they were doing something and the way they did it was a bit wild. No nets.

There are all these moments that have become the moments in VidPop history. The founding party, the murder, the wake, the fight. All good moments. It can't be that everyone who was alive in the seventies and living in Montréal was present for those things but it sure seems like that sometimes.

CÉCILE GRONDIN The evening where Maurice made psychedelic patterns out of Carl-Yves's images was my introduction to VidPop. I went to a screening and a fight broke out. Or I went to a fight and a video screening broke out, as the old hockey joke goes.

I was on the board of Vidéo Populaire for seven years, from 1978-1985. I took the minutes. I always did because I knew shorthand since I'd gone to secretarial school. You have to remember how things were back then. It was good to have those skills because it was not easy to get work as a woman in the seventies. Guess where you ended up? Waitress, secretary, *commis* in a store. Lydia was so happy because she wasn't the only woman anymore. There was me, Esther Fortin and her and we would sometimes just look at each other during meetings and raise our eyebrows and smile.

The founding members had special status in that there was one spot reserved for them on the board and they would rotate each year. When it was Lydia's turn on the board things were pretty smooth, functional. We got stuff done. When it was Carl he really dominated discussions or even hijacked them. But I saw where he was coming from. Things moved, too, but I wouldn't say 'smooth.' When it was Maurice, we began the meetings without him more often than not. If I remember correctly, Terrence took over Maurice's spot on the board because we complained we had no input from the founders and that wasn't good. If Maurice came at all, he would have some piece of equipment out and he would tinker with it during the meeting, a real *patenteur*. Different styles.

RÉAL COUTU We were so committed. I learned that there, being devoted to a cause. There were lots of points of view, not everyone was towing the party line. We were a bit stereotyped as rigid political types but I always wondered how that could be. It wasn't coming from someone who had been to VidPop events, I thought. There were a few put-down names floating around. One was *Vidéo Communiste*. Some of us were communists so we didn't register that as a criticism. You only had to show up to an event or some meeting to see the range of what was going on. I always thought the threat to the organization was from the outside. There was a rumour that the cops were watching us because we were doing work with different causes and were very visible.

ESTHER FORTIN I knew Cécile. She took me to Vidéo Populaire. Lydia was pushing to have more women involved at the board level. I was studying at *École des hautes études commerciales* back then, one of two women in the whole program. I arrived at Vidéo Populaire at a time when it wasn't just about the four founders anymore. There were growing pains for sure. Carl-Yves was not happy when he found out where and what I was studying. He called me 'la fonctionnaire.'

PIERRE NADEAU It was a good place for a loser like me to feel un-loser. I didn't have a problem with Carl-Yves. I shared his political views back then. I wonder if we would share views now? If I had a problem with anyone, it was Terry, but I'm not saying I did have a problem with him. He was often too timid, too much the voice of reason. I liked the energy of a good argument.

I was followed once. I swear it was plainclothes police. Who else? A rival video gang? We were on the radar. I would take the metro to Sherbrooke and walk over to St-Laurent. Two guys, all along Prince-Arthur, staying one block behind me but stopping when I stopped and such. I didn't tell Maurice. You didn't tell him stuff like that. I told Carl and he told me I was *parano*. Then he told me not to tell Maurice and we went back out to see if we could find those two guys.

The video camera was our way to create a new society. Lydia and I became close. She and I talked about all the issues being left out of mainstream media. We did some research together for a video on images of women in advertising. We didn't end up making it but we would meet for coffee and talk about things like that. 'À l'attaque,' as Carl used to say.

LUISA SEPÚLVEDA I came to Québec in 1976 with my brother Lorenzo from Chile. Our father basically said, That's it, pack up, you're going, it's too terrible, too violent here. I met Cécile because of the French class that Lorenzo and I took as new arrivals. She had another Chilean refugee staying at her place. We weren't the only ones. I met so many Chileans in Montréal. Cécile suggested we come to Vidéo Populaire to meet people and practice our French. We went. We were so amazed that such a group could have the right to operate, could do and say what they wanted. It became part of our lives.

LORENZO SEPÚLVEDA No one could believe what had happened, what was still happening in Chile, not even us.

Something had to be done. I wanted to work on something with my sister about what was going on and about the resistance. Vidéo Populaire was supportive. Carl-Yves said it was our story, not theirs, they could help and they would, but it would be my and my sister's project.

LUISA SEPÚLVEDA It took me a while to understand that we were safe. That we could criticize. Be ourselves. When we were younger, Lorenzo and I made several Super 8 films with our father's camera, short horror films mostly. Lorenzo asked me to play in them sometimes. In 1971, we made a horror film *Danza de los espiritus* about ghosts that haunt a landowner. I wrote the script and played one of the main ghosts. Lorenzo did the camera. We edited it together.

LORENZO SEPÚLVEDA Carl-Yves and Maurice wanted to see our films. Maurice had a Super 8 projector and he brought it to Vidéo Populaire so we could look at these movies Luisa and I made as kids. I was so nervous to show them. The last time I'd watched them was back home with my friends.

CÉCILE GRONDIN When Lorenzo and Luisa showed their films to us one evening...it wasn't a public screening. It was Terry, Maurice, Carl-Yves, Lydia and, I think, Pierre and me. Dr. Tim maybe. Maurice showed one of his own Super 8 films that he made when he was a teenager, to break the ice. I don't remember it at all. But I remember the Sepúlvedas' movie. We watched it about five times in a row. Maurice was fascinated.

MAURICE AUBERT I showed my film first. It was so terrible. It was supposed to be a comedy like Buster Keaton. Not even close. People running after each other. Film is not my medium. For me, it's video. I'm embarrassed to say I once thought my film was funny. I figured Carl would unload all his criticism on my movie, call it unoriginal, which it was, and leave Luisa and Lorenzo and their films alone.

Their films were so much better than mine. One of them was wonderful. Lorenzo is a great cameraman. In one shot, Luisa appears next to a pond that has mist on it. They shot in these ruins just outside of Iquique. She comes toward the camera from the background. She's not floating, but it almost looks like she is. I got chills.

TERRENCE O'MEARA   It reminded me of *Carnival of Souls*.

LYDIA CARTWRIGHT   That happened to us quite often, people like the Sepúlvedas joining us for a time and keeping us focused, channelling VidPop towards a cause. Carl-Yves and Terry were adamant: the four of us made videos about things that affected us directly, but that didn't mean we couldn't help directors with personal projects.

We were reading things on imperfect cinema and trying to see lots of documentaries.

CARL-YVES DUBÉ   Their film was political. It was about the dictatorship.

LORENZO SEPÚLVEDA   There was no going home for us, not for a long time, but we were invited to this place and these people greeted us like friends. When I used to hear people say Vidéo Populaire was insular or like a club, I would tell them what I thought.

MAURICE AUBERT   I got very excited by their film. These people, all ages, men and women, children too, leave their graves and walk slowly out to the fields where they begin working like it was just another day for them. The landowner rides up on his horse and gets the shock of his life, because some of them worked for his grandfather and father when he was a child. Some of the people have been dead for fifty years and there they are, working.

CÉCILE GRONDIN   I stayed involved for so long because of the people I met there. Luisa and Lorenzo contributed to VidPop. And everyone was excited. The idea of politics expanded. It was good for me, for us, to be around people who were fighting different causes. We were committed to video as an art form. We were, most of us, for the independence of Québec. We wanted some kind of revolution. I was personally wary of communism, which I think is a great system but always in the hands of imperfect people...But we wanted major change.

ESTHER FORTIN I stayed for a few years. It wasn't a good fit. I liked many of the people. Cécile and I are still friends. I admit I thought the place was going nowhere. I'm going to describe a typical meeting to you. Lydia and Terrence, *impeccable*, prepared, ready to work. Maurice...he always sat a bit away from the table with a piece of equipment in his lap. He was always cleaning or repairing something. He never looked up. He never said a word. Carl-Yves also sat a bit away from the table, with his arms crossed, and he said a lot. He cut people off. If anyone tried to restore order, Carl-Yves would accuse them of being square and wanting to mimic corporate culture. Those remarks were directed at me for sure.

PIERRE NADEAU My first video started as a conversation with Rosemary. We would mock argue all the time. I thought she was so Anglophone with such an Anglo name and a terrible accent when she spoke French. And she would tease me about my English, which was pathetic. We decided it would be funny to make a video on the subject. We shot both of us talking to the camera, reading the same text, me in French, her in English. Rosemary took off for California after we got the footage. I put her name on the video but I did all the editing. Reactions were mixed. Carl didn't see the point. Now it's considered a kind of classic.

LYDIA CARTWRIGHT Always. Always the main question. Why did Maurice go? The second one is why did Carl-Yves leave? Never, ever, why did I leave or why did Terry stay?

Or why did other people get involved for a while and then leave? Because it's normal. Because that's how things go. Those can't be the defining moments of Vidéo Populaire, the departures.

The reason I used to hear first was that 'politics' broke us up. Politics. Not a vast or nuanced subject at all. Another reason was the rumour about Laurent, Carl-Yves and Maurice. Murderers! Third reason I've heard was about Maurice being art and Carl being agit-prop. And the best one as far as I'm concerned was that Terry and me kicked the two others out because we wanted Vidéo Populaire to go mainstream, corporate. Seriously.

It is more complicated than personal conflicts and political ideologies. No one seriously suggested that Maurice be asked to leave or even that he be given limited access. I think people were frustrated. Moe had a reputation for making people wait when they had booked equipment. This is one time where I think maybe Terry didn't see the big picture. He was more lenient, more forgiving of Moe. We had to start thinking about what we wanted to offer. We even had to start thinking ahead, planning for the future. We got through the first phase by the skin of our teeth. Now, we had to figure out a five-year plan. None of us thought like that. We didn't know what strategic planning was. We had members to think about and visiting artists. It wasn't just us four anymore.

TERRENCE O'MEARA Maurice said to me once he thought he was pushed out. I was so disturbed by him saying that because I always felt that he was the heart of us. And that we did everything to accommodate him. No one ever asked him to leave. Sure, I sometimes got fed up with him and his popcorn sandwiches. He could be a handful but I loved the guy. After the first three years of VidPop, he never came to the meetings. Never cleaned up or contributed coffee money. He just shot and edited and tried to bump other people out of the edit suite so he could stay longer.

No, that's not true, he didn't try to bump people, he just basically stayed put until he won or they did.

MAURICE AUBERT I was making VidPop's name back then. People wanted to see my work. I wasn't always editing. I tried to do a lot of my work at night to keep out of the way. They told me my presence had to be more than me shooting and editing. It also had to be accessible to other artists. They told me I had to try and be there in different ways. I tried. I did.

CÉCILE GRONDIN It was something the board talked about often at a certain point. We had equipment that was state of the art at the time. People wanted to use it. Members. Also people who I guess you would call clients, who had no link to VidPop apart from wanting to shoot or edit videos. We had trouble making rent sometimes and it would have made sense to take paying customers but that was a whole difficult discussion. The fact that Maurice was camped out in the editing room when others had deadlines was a hard thing to deal with. But to be fair he was not there all the time, it was in phases.

CARL-YVES DUBÉ I hate waiting. I'm sure I threw some fits. Others did, too. I even made up a sign to hang over the Vidéo Populaire one on the door. It read 'Bureau de Maurice Aubert.' If things got out of hand, I would tape it over our real sign. I obviously wasn't there when he left the centre.

I never thought that the reception of Maurice's work went to his head. He was getting accolades even early on. He just had to keep going. If he stopped, it wasn't good. I understood that on some level. I was the same way but for different reasons. He didn't do it to piss people off or because he thought he was this amazing artist that deserved recognition. It was hard because we were free-form back then. Open all the time, no official job titles for us as employees. And suddenly we are thinking and talking about curtailing Maurice's access. I was often so conflicted because I thought we were becoming corporate but I was also irritated by Maurice's habits.

I used to look under the table at his feet to check his socks and shoes, because they were sometimes mismatched.

LYDIA CARTWRIGHT Maurice never knew what was going on if he was working on something. Staff and members would come and go, board meetings would take place and he was oblivious. No. Not oblivious. Detached. Oh, I don't know if that's the right word either. Don't ask him about dates or names. You won't get anywhere. Ask him about cameras and editing machines and videos he likes. He was our equipment archivist, keeping and organizing all the operating manuals. He would pull out the old cameras once a week to run a check on them. Amazing.

ESTHER FORTIN I was the scapegoat. There was all this talk about Maurice and how amazing his videos were but the truth was he was keeping lots of potential paying customers away. I pointed out that we were often behind in paying rent. I wasn't the only one looking at that. Several of them — Terry, Lydia, Cécile and others — told me Maurice was in a way costing the centre money. Even Carl-Yves complained. I brought it up at a meeting. Carl-Yves told me to take my right-wing commercial opinions elsewhere. So I did and I resigned.

TERRENCE O'MEARA Moe missed all the plans we were making. He missed discussions when it was time to update equipment. We only had one closed room for editing and it didn't have room for the new and old machines. We tried a few things. We set the old equipment up in the larger office area because we had the space. Not ideal, but Moe just couldn't work. He needed the same room he was used to. And he needed the same machines. I think he couldn't deal with any change. He would come in and slump down on a chair. I would make him coffee and try to talk to him about the new set-up. You can get used to it, I said over and over. It was like he woke up then, like he realized it wasn't 1976 anymore. Marcel, an early member, was gone, punching the clock in a factory. 'When did he leave?' Lydia was doing her M.A. in Women's Studies and spending a little less time at the centre. We weren't taping every demonstration or protest. We weren't doing tons of drugs. We were still collaborating on each other's projects but not as much. Carl was gone.

Maurice was not kicked out. He stopped coming. This would be 1985 or so. I never asked for his keys. Twice, I found popcorn on the floor when I came in in the morning. Did he come to the office just to sit and think? On those mornings when I saw the popcorn, I thought he might be coming back, that he had some things he wanted to try out, that he was working on something new. The second time I knew it couldn't have been him because we'd moved and he didn't have the new keys. I was all hopeful until I realized.

We moved the old machines and old cameras into a corner. We had to make room for the new editing equipment. We have a Sony Portapak. It's beautiful. We never purchased it for VidPop. An artist who didn't want to store it at his place gave it to us. I probably loved that camera more for what it promised than what it actually delivered. But oh my, to have held one for the first time, heavy, figuring it out and thinking 'here we go.' I've never had that since. I loved the Portapak best. We had all the cameras, one after the other in quick succession. The first one we bought was a Sony AVC-3400 Vidicon Portapak. I don't have that good a memory. Maurice insisted we keep every piece of equipment. And we pretty much have. No other art form has as many 'dead' formats as video. Now we are mulling over which HD camera to purchase. It's a pain in the ass, frankly. I know it isn't the best approach but I tend to wait and see which format will 'win' the market.

DVDs make me crazy. I find myself ranting about the fragility of the format in every class I teach. Information falls off DVDs all the time. In some ways I would rather take my chance with a VHS tape. The number of times I've put a DVD on to play and nothing happens. Or it happens badly.

CARL-YVES DUBÉ   I'm saying this and I want this in. If it doesn't go in, let me know right now because I will revoke my permission, okay? I won't be portrayed as the only bad guy. I had my ideas and I think they are defensible.

I used to work at a depanneur making deliveries. At the same time, I was a bagger at a grocery store. Two shit jobs with low wages. I used to finish work and run to Vidéo Populaire in those early years. I couldn't wait to get there.

I did my time there and then it was done. Things didn't turn out the way we wanted. The new social order never came. Not even close. For me, Vidéo Populaire was part of that, a way to bring social change. When you're in it, you aren't thinking 'naïve,' you are just going. By 1981 the cards were on the table. I could see that no amount of good work on our part was going to do a fucking thing. The fact that we lost the Referendum in 1980 was a huge loss, but I still felt hopeful.

No matter what the others say or how I come across, I was there, fully there, from 1974-1981. There was nothing else. Seven years is huge. *Rashomon*. It should be required viewing. It says a lot about how memory works.

MARC DELORME   I became a *membre-associé* in 1976 or maybe early 1977. I was nineteen. It was the year of the Montréal Olympics or right after. I was a volunteer at the Centre Paul-Sauvé. I saw these guys outside of the venue. They had a camera and a big mic and were trying to get interviews with people going in and out of the arena. They didn't look like regular TV guys. Carl-Yves and Maurice had a lot of hair. We had cigarettes together and Carl-Yves told me about Vidéo Populaire. They were doing a video about the cleanup of Montréal for the Olympics, which I hadn't even heard about, the sweep of the red light district and stuff like that. Carl told me I should be more informed and to drop by if I was interested and wanted to know more. I did. In 1979 I became an employee and started working as the...I guess the first distribution employee. It was just VidPop videos at first. So I became a *membre-travailleur*.

LYDIA CARTWRIGHT I thought we should start thinking about getting our work out into the world. Our videos needed to circulate. There were more and more video festivals and also film festivals adding video sections. Marc took it on.

MARC DELORME I felt like I was out of my depth. Terry was nice, he would always tell me that they all felt that way. I think it was just thirty or so tapes at first, the entire collection. It was works by the four of them and also ones by Pierre, Antonio, Rosemary and artists who did co-productions or productions at VidPop. Our catalogue was done with a typewriter and Letraset and photocopied. The tapes were all kinds of formats. So big compared to now. One of the first things we did was to watch all the videos and write descriptions for them together.

CARL-YVES DUBÉ Maurice and I worked hard on the tape about the Olympics. We never quite finished it. We had a version I liked and a version he liked. My version contained all the stuff about how much the games cost, how much the stadium cost us all, about the scummy politics and corruption and the total waste. The Olympic Stadium has never stopped being a joke. Maurice was making montage sections with images of Montréal.

ROSEMARY DRUMMOND That Olympic tape took on mythical proportions. The two of them just couldn't figure it out. It went on and on. They usually worked together really well. There was some good stuff there. I certainly saw it enough times in different versions. Just fucking finish it already. Carl-Yves could have rammed through his vision, no contest. Maurice wasn't a pushover but he would have done what Carl said. So Carl didn't always try to get his way. There is a rumour that the tape is finished but that they never released it.

MARC DELORME Carl had me put the description for their Olympic video in the distribution catalogue for 1979. The title was *Montréal 1976*. So it went in. But it never got finished. The 1979 catalogue is a bit of a collector's item I guess because it has this mistake.

TERRENCE O'MEARA Judging from the calls and requests we got, that tape would have been a hit...if you can say hit for independent videos. I got in a huge fight with Carl, surprise, surprise, because I thought they should name their video something else. It dated the tape, 1976, and this was 1978 or 1979 when they were trying to finish it. Carl thought my suggestion was an example of my commercial thinking.

MAURICE AUBERT Carl could show up and I could show him my version.

LYDIA CARTWRIGHT When Marc left, we didn't have the resources to pay someone to take on distribution so I did it for a few years. We had new titles, probably close to eighty in all. I was tempted to leave in *Montréal 1976*, as an homage to Carl and Maurice, but of course I didn't. I guess I was in charge of distribution for more like six or seven years. The next person who took care of distribution was Roger Cross. We opened things up. We started taking work that was not produced at VidPop. When Roger was hired, there were maybe over two hundred videos.

CÉCILE GRONDIN I never allowed myself to say it back then but when Carl-Yves left, VidPop was free. He was so rigid. The Olympics tape is a good example. They had something, him and Maurice, a good video. But it wasn't perfect or somehow didn't correspond to Carl's ideas so he shelved it.

ROSEMARY DRUMMOND The others won't be good for the record here, none of them. They were right in it, holding their positions and lobbing bombs at each other. What can you remember in those circumstances? It was late 1981. Carl wasn't even that mad at Terry, Maurice or Lydia. If anything, he was mad at me because I was meeting people and occasionally turning them on to VidPop. I wasn't saying, hey, come on in, make yourself at home, make any video about anything you like, but I thought the place needed more than us. He thought it was all changing for the bad. He wanted to keep things the same. He would glare at me if I walked in with new people.

ANTONIO DUTTO I know that people can't and won't always stay. I don't have any illusions that way. I really questioned Carl about his decision to leave Vidéo Populaire because I asked him why and he said it wasn't really a decision, it was a feeling. Fair enough, great. What feeling was it? He couldn't say. Man, when I heard that. If it wasn't a decision and it wasn't a feeling, then how did he figure it out? He also didn't tell me for like a year. I kept in touch with Terry and Lydia sporadically and they didn't tell me, either, but I wasn't surprised because they were respectful of Carl. He would tell me to stop being romantic about it, but I don't think I was being the romantic one.

I called VidPop once and Maurice answered. I should have bought a lottery ticket that day because he never answers the phone. Maurice. He reminded me of my brother in some ways. We talked about this and that. I'm sure I did most of the talking but I eventually asked if Carl was there and he said 'He's around but I don't see him right now.' This was after Carl had left to never come back. He didn't see him right now!

DAVID SUMMERVILLE Everybody talks about the implosion like it happened last week. I kind of hung with Dr. Tim and Pierre at that time. We would go to Tim's office and talk about how things were going south.

At one point, I thought 'that's it, they're all going.' The idea floating around was to get board members and some active members involved so the centre itself wouldn't shut down. It was crisis mode. But in the end it was only Carl-Yves.

Tim tried talking to Carl-Yves. They got along great. Who knows why. Just one of those weird people combinatations that worked. Tim said Carl was mixing VidPop up with all the other disappointments he was feeling and he couldn't unravel the strands. Tim tried and tried to get through to Carl.

LYDIA CARTWRIGHT I felt like a fraud sometimes. Terry and I were representing something that had been founded by four people. As of the mid-eighties, two were MIA. We agonized over that. One thing I thought of this morning was that it never even occured to us then to make a statement or write a press release or anything like that. If someone left a centre they founded now, that would be the first consideration. It was a different time for sure.

There would be hundreds of people to contact for this. Lots of turnover in a centre where you don't have great pay or much job security. Board members lasted longer than staff. I think we had a member who did twelve or more years. Staff often average about two to three years. Terry would know more than me.

Terry calls me 'the consience' but it is really him. I worry about leaving someone out and I can describe them but he mostly remembers their names. And if he doesn't, there are paper trails.

Dr. Tim. In a way he is a VidPop success story because he was a friendly guy who dropped in and kind of hung out off and on. He still comes to the occasional screening. We had no money then and Dr. Tim took me on as a patient in exchange for workshops or something. Terry, too. Even Carl liked him and would present him 'et ça c'est notre dentiste, Dr. Tim' to get reactions.

DR. TIMOTHY PETERSON Terry and Lydia are still my patients! I'm preparing my retirement, a little behind schedule.

When I still had my office there, I took a camera workshop with Maurice. Lovely man, so gentle. I did learn a lot. But he started the workshop by having everybody just cradle the camera kind of like a baby. I was already a fish out of water there, a dentist with all these counter-culture types. I held it like a baby thinking 'okay, now what' and felt completely self-conscious. Then Maurice took us through how he did things, shot things and we all taped little segments and we made a pretty far-out short video out of that workshop. I didn't get the bug or anything but I enjoyed myself.

I went up to Carl and told him that he and I shouldn't ever talk politics because I would come off as conservative when I wasn't really. He liked that. I thought he was a passionate guy, very committed and smart. We became friends.

When he left, I told him I would not let him disappear. He sure has tried to. We see each other maybe not as often as I'd like.

ROSAIRE LACHANCE I got a press release at the community radio station that it was the 10th anniversary of Vidéo Populaire. I guess that would be mid-eighties? I was interested in having someone in to talk about what they were up to. I was surprised that three of the original members showed up. That guy Carl-Yves was gone. Maurice though, he was there but almost like he was absent, too. I thought it was odd three people show up and one of them could have just not bothered. The other two did all the talking. Maurice looked down at the floor. I showed him the technical set-up in the studio. I remember he loved machines. It occurred to me that maybe he needed to be with the two others.

TERRENCE O'MEARA One day I came in to find the pile of old machines and tables gone. Nothing else was taken. And the lock hadn't been forced. I was freaked out. 1986, I think. Him, Maurice! It had to be. Nothing else was touched. I was the only one who was happy. Some of the others thought we should press charges. Mostly encouraged by Coutu, Réal

Coutu, a board member. We had bought the equipment for the centre and it should stay on the premises. But no one uses it anymore. Doesn't matter. Part of our archives. Part of our history. I could see the point of that. I disagreed with pressing charges, but agreed that the equipment should come back to the centre.

We weren't even sure it was Maurice, but I was designated to go to see him and tell him the equipment was a loan. I didn't mind being given the assignment. What I minded was the utter desolation I felt. I remember thinking Moe had gotten it right. He had left at the right time. With the right equipment. He was a pain, but he got his exit just right. And I got mine all wrong. And I would continue to get it wrong. And Carl-Yves. I thought about him, too.

I went to his apartment on Coloniale. I knocked because the doorbell was broken. It had never worked, not even when he first moved in. I thought he might not answer. But he did.

He opened the door. Said nothing.

'Hey Maurice. Just need to verify that you have the equipment from VidPop. Coutu thought it was stolen. But I figured it was you. Was it?'

It wasn't a smile. It was just the two corners of his mouth squiggling.

'Did he want to have me arrested?'

'He was pretty angry.'

'But you talked him out of it.'

'Yes. And came to tell you the equipment is a loan. It should return to VidPop.'

'It's OB. SO. LETE.'

'We bought it for VidPop!'

'VidPop is gone.'

'No, Moe, you're gone. You left. You could have stayed. But you just left.'

'You should too.'

Those words. I got angry. I don't remember what else I said, but I think I told him he abandoned the cause and that VidPop was still useful, still pertinent. I convinced myself then and there. My own raised voice. My blood pressure rising. Both up, up.

'You can keep the equipment until you finish your tape.'

The squiggling mouth again.

'And then you bring it back. Whatever we decide, it is for us to decide.' I hated my pompous tone. Coutu, I thought, would have punched him.

Moe looked right into my eyes, a pretty rare thing. He said 'The fish are drowning, comrade.' He shut the door.

I yelled through the wood. 'What the fuck does that mean?' But I knew exactly what he meant. I knew it but ignored it.

It was a long time ago, but I remember my walk back to VidPop. I was fired up. Goodbye to our Marxist roots (to be fair, some of us were Trotskyites). It had been a desolate walk to his house, but I remember feeling a bit giddy.

VidPop was going on. Two founding members were not involved, but I for one intended to stay and fight. I don't know when I saw Moe again after that. Might have been almost a year.

MAURICE AUBERT I tracked down Marcel Blouin and he helped me move these machines from the centre to here. Two trips. He had a car from the seventies, a Buick or something. Huge, like a boat, it would take up two parking spots now. Carl-Yves talked and talked about the workers and the revolution. Marcel actually lived it. He became a worker. He gave up his membership in VidPop and went to work in a factory. We lost touch over the years. The last time I saw him, he was a union guy and still working in the same place. Late eighties. He's gone now. He was just a few years older than me. I'll always be really grateful that he helped me get this stuff over here. He loved the idea that we were liberating machines that were being put out to pasture.

I stopped going. Carl was gone. It took me a while to understand he was not coming back. I was having trouble getting there. And I thought it was time to go somehow even though I loved it. I loved us. I was waiting for a sign. Then I realized I'd been waiting for a sign for two years. That was sign enough. Terry took it personally. It took him a long time to see. As much as I've thought about it, all I can really say is that I had this awful metallic feeling, this sharp silver feeling, almost like a touch, that pointed me out the door.

RÉAL COUTU   Maurice was so entitled. He just took the machines without a word. I didn't care that no one was using them.

I was a delivery driver for a chicken chain back then. Going to Vidéo Populaire was a welcome change. I felt like I was doing something interesting because the rest of the time it seemed I was stuck at traffic lights smelling greasy chicken and french fries. You would think that Carl-Yves would have been more supportive. Here I was this other Québécois working-class guy trying to pay rent, but he had to remind me I was working for an evil company and bringing unhealthy food to oppressed people who didn't know better. He hammered everyone. Called me 'Monsieur Poulet.'

I credit being on the board with helping me get a job I actually liked. I met some people who were into what VidPop stood for. They told me about an MDJ (Maison des jeunes) that needed a coordinator. I got that job and it led to lots of other jobs in the same field over the years.

TERRENCE O'MEARA   My hair left my head in waves. Slowly but steadily. Very much like my pure Marxist convictions. Most of my comrades were long gone. I'm still a socialist. I vote Québec solidaire provincially and NDP federally. I used to vote PQ provincially. Not that any of the parties I support correspond to my idea of socialism, but anyhow, better than the alternatives. I go see Dr. Tim for my checkups and we talk about things like that and how so much has changed. I asked the board if I could make Dr. Tim an honorary member. They said yes and I told him and he was so thrilled.

I was given an award in recognition of my 'contribution to the video medium' in 2004. I'm sure I got it because I was the last one standing from VidPop. There was no one else around to honour. No one that would show up. I tried really hard to get Maurice and Lydia to attend with me. He couldn't do it. Lydia was away on sabbatical. She sent me an e-mail and I read her words when I accepted the award. I also tried to get in touch with Carl-Yves. Nothing. I edited some excerpts together, bits of videos by each of us and one of our collaborations so I wouldn't feel so alone up there accepting the award.

NORMAND CÔTÉ I went to Vidéo Populaire in the first years to get some help making a documentary on literacy. Part of the process it seemed was that you would screen your work-in-progress and people would criticize your work. I didn't mind but it went on forever. It was a process of *autocritique*. I'm guessing it was called self-criticism in English. There was a sign on the wall at VidPop. It read *'Pratiquer courageusement la critique et l'autocritique.'* People were supposed to take apart their own videos. I think I remember being told I wasn't going far enough. That video, the one on literacy, was a contract for a centre that worked on that issue. I had to put certain things in the video like an interview with the coordinator. The Vidéo Populaire staff was trying to get me to do a parallel video to the contract, something that was by me on the same subject but not controlled by money. Mao was a big influence. Also, I kind of sidestepped the whole Marxist-Leninist cell thing. Wasn't interested. I was always kind of amazed that all these people were reading these dry communist texts.

TERRENCE O'MEARA We didn't have bad intentions. I try to forgive myself. After all the *autocritique*, a kind of absolution. See, I would have been in trouble saying something like that back then because you did not mix your Mao with religious references.

CARL-YVES DUBÉ No one was tortured into changing their videos. The idea was for each director to reflect on their work in a spirit of complete honesty. I know the process helped me very much. One guy called it 'video by committee.'

NORMAND CÔTÉ I called them 'Vidéo Pop-Tarts' behind their backs. I didn't want my own work to come out of something so rigid. I liked a lot of movie directors and thought what is the problem if I watch a Capra movie? But it was a problem for some of them. I stopped going. I ended up forming my own production company in 1982.

MAURICE AUBERT After the first few times, I just couldn't. It was too hard. I never had a thing to say. Some of those images that people were identifying as problematic I found beautiful. What was the big problem if someone had a beautiful shot of a tree?

LYDIA CARTWRIGHT We saw it as part of our duties as founding members. I actually don't remember when it stopped for good or when I stopped participating. I'm sure we told some artist-producers that some of their images were counter-revolutionary or something like that. Maurice had a hard time with it. He couldn't do it. He just didn't feel that it was our place to tell people what they should or should not put in their work. It wasn't just us four, though. Sometimes the group would be made up of *membres-producteurs* or staff. Over time, we evolved a mentoring program at VidPop. It is still part of our services. We have a deadline once a year. If you are an emerging artist, you can apply to work with an established artist. I kind of think of that program as a positive legacy of that more...rigorous process.

I have one video called *Apprécier la vidéo* (How to appreciate vidéo)...I did a performance in which I eat videotape. I had a feeling about those images and how they might be perceived so I shot the video in secret, not telling anyone. That was hard to do because it seemed like

74

there was always someone at VidPop. I would just stay until Maurice finally left, then haul the camera out and do my thing. Carl was kind of amazed when he saw it. He forgot himself and asked me what tape tasted like. Not very good, by the way, the taste, kind of metallic scotch tapey, but more intense and musty. You could really taste the chemicals. Then he remembered himself and asked me what I was saying, that video was another product that could be easily consumed? I said that it was about issues around eating and body image. Carl wasn't too keen but if I remember correctly, others saw the value. When Dr. Tim saw that work, his mouth was literally hanging open in the shape of a perfect 'o.' He chastised me about doing that kind of thing, because it was bad for my teeth not to mention my overall health.

ROSEMARY DRUMMOND I actually convinced Carl-Yves to work with me on one of my videos. I started getting grey hairs really young, in my early twenties. I did this one performance where I would ask for volunteers to come and pluck the grey hairs right off my head. When I decided to do it as a video performance, I wanted Carl to be the one person doing the plucking. It's called *Hair (Less)*. I worked on him for weeks. I used the terms and language I thought would get him on board. I wanted it to be a man because of sexism, oppression and misogyny. Finally he said okay and we shot for twenty minutes. You don't see his face, just him from shoulders to hips and his hands going through my hair, locating the grey and yanking. Sometimes he was delicate. Sometimes not. I asked him to vary. We had a lot of fun but it didn't stop him from being critical, telling me my performance was derivative.

It was strategic in a way. How could Carl-Yves object to something he agreed to be in?

CÉCILE GRONDIN I participated in a few of those sessions. They have kind of been mythologized but weren't as bad as the stories, at least not the ones I sat in on. Things like 'why do you feel that shot is necessary?' It was more of a conversation.

NANCY AMIOT I would have loved to be a fly on the wall at one of those. Can you imagine? Terry and Lydia will talk about it but they seem maybe a bit reluctant. The one to talk to would be Carl-Yves but that just hasn't been possible.

I've always thought that process represents an interesting rupture with the artist as single creator. *Autocritique* was not only practiced at Vidéo Populaire but was quite a widespread phenomenon and not just in art.

ROSEMARY DRUMMOND It made sense to me, the collective approach. I sat in on a few sessions and it was not 'you can't do this.' Until I was working on a production with Lydia and two other women and Pierre Nadeau said 'that shot seems irrelevant.' In other words, 'you can't do this' and I didn't like that at all.

PIERRE NADEAU I loved those sessions. I loved them for my own work and I always thought they were beneficial for everyone. You didn't like something you saw in a video, you had to learn to formulate your criticism. It wasn't personal.

TERRENCE O'MEARA We kind of gave Maurice dispensation from *autocritique* sessions. Carl-Yves didn't insist too much. Out of all of us, he could see fragility in Moe. And they were tight then.

Moe once told me he travelled by train because he could reach a state of heightened melancholy by staring out the window. Classic Maurice.

When the train pulled into the station, he would rush home, trying to hold on to this blanket of sadness and nostalgia. He got into these conditions of intense feeling that he would try to transmit to his videos. Osmosis. You had to be a little crazy, I guess, a little out there to think you could make your tape sad by being sad. Here's the thing. He made people sad. You watched his work and there was a sadness, a feeling that enveloped you. It didn't come from the content. It just came. When I watched his video *No 9*, I was reminded of a train trip I had taken years before. I'd forgotten all about it, it was just Montréal to Québec City, but he brought it back. I had just been dumped by Philippa and was not coping well. I drank a lot of Carlsberg and stared out the window. The conductor came and asked for tickets. I couldn't find mine right away. He waited patiently, looking away from me because I had been crying. His nametag. R. Gervais. See, Moe made me remember all that. Other things, too. It's like he was practicing alchemy or something. His videos, especially *No 3*, *No 5* and *No 13* all provoked reactions in viewers. At one screening I remember, one guy rose to his feet and said 'Yes, yes' to the screen. I remember looking at the screen then to see what he was agreeing with and it was an out of focus image of Moe's dog, Viking. People were always standing and saying something during his videos. They were laughing or crying or they would put their heads in their hands or stand. I expected these reactions but I never got used to them.

You can imagine what I felt. I was the last one from VidPop so it fell to me to travel with his videos. He wouldn't. He never would. He would say yes, then never show up, which added to his reputation. I felt like a fraud, introducing his work, his collection of compelling abstractions that moved people to say and do things. I would introduce the videos by telling people that they might experience some effects. Spectators would smirk or look at me like I was *mal vissé*... had a screw loose. Then they would watch and someone in the audience would do or say something during the screening. Not every time, mind you, but often enough. Afterwards, they would want to know things. Where was he now? Did he still make work? Would it be possible to meet him? I would give my pat answers. People would like me a bit more because I had some information on Moe.

He kept the equipment. Coutu was so pissed off that we weren't pressing charges he threatened to leave the board or maybe even left the board. I think Maurice maintained the machines as best he could. And I do think he continued making videos on formats that no one could play anymore. Maurice is okay for money. His folks left him and his sister some. Which is good because Maurice can't work eight hours a day, five days a week.

I became the conservator of Maurice Aubert's videos. I always tell him about screenings, turnout, details about the room, who I met, like that. He knows his work is out there being shown to all kinds of people.

One year, there were so many screenings for his videos that VidPop made some good money. Sixty per cent of all money generated from sales and rentals was Moe's. I would instruct the accountant to send Moe his cheques. They were never cashed. I got this idea one year. I thought I would buy him a computer and load it with Final Cut Pro and other programs so he could make his videos. I was so happy about this that I made several attempts to see him. I went to his place on Coloniale regularly for several weeks. I would try in the mornings, afternoons and evenings. Random. He was home. He is pretty much always home. I tried calling, too, but the phone just rang and rang. I pictured his phone, a black rotary dial sitting on a cluttered desk. He had never been much for phone conversations anyhow and had probably been fighting with the phone company to keep the old model. He liked what he liked and he liked obsolete things. He could make them work, take them apart, see them for what they were. I eventually had to give up on the computer idea.

PHILIPPA JOHNSON Terrence and I were together for about four years. I broke up with him because of Vidéo Populaire. I know that probably sounds horrible. I liked the place and I supported the politics, but Terrence just disappeared into it, got swallowed up, you know? Also, I was seeing myself clearly for maybe the first time, how I had never been single and somehow every current boyfriend's activities became mine. Terry helped me put an end to that in a way.

Years later I was able to tell him I was grateful for that and he was okay with it.

We were together for two years before they began their set-up. I remember that Maurice's girlfriend Marie and I joked about being 'VidPop widows.' After they moved out of his apartment down to the first office, Terrence sometimes slept there. At least I knew where he was, but I just started not caring. Our entire social life became that place. A date would be me going there, joining Terry and others for a beer and hanging out. They would talk about what needed doing or some project. Sometimes they could finish each other's sentences. My French got really good. Terry and I spoke English together when we were alone but at VidPop it was French.

LYDIA CARTWRIGHT We were compatible on many levels. But our tastes were very different. Terry used to say that VidPop was born the same year as *Black Christmas* and *The Texas Chainsaw Massacre*. The rest of us preferred the fact that *Céline et Julie vont en bateau* and *A Woman Under the Influence* came out the same year. Carl was into *Hearts and Minds*, even though he had serious criticism of it. When didn't he? Sometimes Terry's love of movies and pop culture really made Carl-Yves go ballistic. He couldn't believe that one of his collaborators was wasting his time on trash. He was kind of the high-priest of acceptable actions. You had to check with Carl to have your leisure time vetted. The funny thing was that Carl whistled. It proved that not even he could tune out pop culture completely. You could catch him whistling tunes that he wouldn't have been caught dead listening to, like *My Eyes Adored You* or *Love Will Keep Us Together*. If he made me really, really mad, I would call him on it. When Kate Bush's first album came out, he mangled his way through some of her songs.

We used to bring in the records we were into. It wasn't a regular thing but we would have listening parties, put on an album, see how the others liked it, have a drink.

TERRENCE O'MEARA I used to do it on purpose sometimes, talk about things to get at Carl-Yves. Carl asked me not to talk about musicals or westerns or noirs in our workspace anymore. I was doing it just to bug him. But there was a certain look in his eye so I stopped.

Black Christmas is a really good film. Bob Clark should be remembered for that movie and *Deathdream* instead of *Porky's*. When I saw *Black Christmas* I told Lydia she could have been Kidder's twin. She wasn't impressed. Thinks all horror films are anti-woman.

MAURICE AUBERT Someone says or does something and Terry is comparing it to a movie. He told me to watch *The Conversation*. I did and I think he thought I was like Harry Caul in that movie. All those nice old sound machines and recording techniques and a weird insular loner guy in the middle of this conspiracy.

I'm not against new things. I use new stuff. The old stuff still works and I use it. I've made modifications. I like the feel, the look. I like tape, the smell.

A friend brought me a small HD camera he got. Compared to what we used to pay for cameras, it's really cheap. I'm reading the manual.

I'm up to *No 204* in my tape series. Terry would die if he knew they are sitting here and all those old ones of mine, the ones he knows about, *No 1* to *No 23* are still travelling the world. I don't know if I want them to leave this apartment. Maybe when I'm gone they can go out. We'll see.

The year I turned fifty I saw plenty of ghosts. It was ghost overdrive. I was going to tell Terry but then I thought he might come back with a scene from a movie. They weren't like movie ghosts talking to you, directing you, telling you where you failed. Showing you the way and showering you with love. They just hovered. I felt like trying to call Carl that year. Thinking about him kind of settled me. We haven't talked since 1984. Not too long ago, I heard someone whistling on my street. I went out the front door onto the balcony. For a second I thought it was Carl coming to visit me.

TERRENCE O'MEARA I don't think anyone knows this. I was very close to being the first of us to leave Vidéo Populaire. Philippa had ended things. I was not doing well. And I was convinced that I had blown it all, my relationship with her and my life, because of spending all my time at VidPop. It hadn't happened, the revolution. And it wasn't likely to. And I was worried about Carl-Yves and Maurice. Carl wouldn't talk and Maurice couldn't. I felt like I was just talking all the time and even I wanted to tell myself to shut up.

You know that phase after a breakup where everything seems like it's underwater? Something probably happened to reconnect me to the centre but I'm not sure if it was a project we were developing or what.

After Philippa dumped me, Maurice kept rolling me cigarettes but I had quit by then. It was his way of supporting me. I would find a whole row of neat cigarettes on my workstation in the mornings. I would pass them out to people who still smoked.

DR. TIMOTHY PETERSON It was new for me, different. I looked forward to seeing them and would stop by for coffee. Their office was set up to kind of welcome you in and mine had the typical gatekeeper desk, you know, a receptionist to stop you from advancing. When I decided to move it was because I got a better deal in a nicer building. Parking. All that stuff. I did it but I regretted it. I bowed to pressure. My wife Greta thought it best. I wasn't going to give up being what I was but I missed seeing them.

I went back for video presentations. When Carl-Yves left and then Maurice, I talked often to Terry about how that affected him. I was a total outsider but I felt affection for them and the place. In a way they had taken me in and showed me something that not everyone knew about.

CARL-YVES DUBÉ I now mark Tim moving his office as the beginning of the end.

PHILLIPA JOHNSON They could scream and yell at each other but resented anyone else trying that out on them. I was an insider but an outsider, too. Terry and Lydia were evolving into the administrators of the place. Terry was taking on the day-to-day functioning. Lydia was looking at other models of centres and grants. Distribution, too. Carl-Yves was overseeing productions, the group's own and other artists'. Maurice was a funny one. I liked him very much but I told Terry that he was...I dont't think I used the word deadweight but that was how it was interpreted. I was enough of an insider to be able to see that and to say it. But Terry got very angry with me, told me I was being unfair. Suddenly, three of them were mad at me. The only person who wasn't mad at me was Maurice.

CÉCILE GRONDIN I remember some meetings were interminable. We would have an agenda with a set number of points and we would follow the *Code Morin* to the letter. When we got to Varia, though, all kinds of subjects would come up. Was the *Code Morin* too restrictive, fascist even? That was one argument. Were we falling into a trap by using it? Was everyone being heard? And so on.

We needed to purchase a new camera. The type of camera became important. Which camera was the best for the needs of Vidéo Populaire members? But the manufacturer of the camera had to be the most proletarian. We wanted to buy something that was less corporate, more progressive. Which was better in terms of human rights and such: Sony or Panasonic? Maurice and Carl-Yves went on about actually building their own camera. It was a Marxist thing.

That Carl was...I'll say semi-convinced...there was a feminist agenda to take over the centre. I was on the board. Who else? Esther (Fortin). Two women and five men and we were supposedly pushing the guys out. One thing

Vidéo Populaire needed was someone to do the accounting. I suggested a woman who had worked at this women's centre. Carl refused to consider her. He was the political radical who was really conservative I think because he wanted to keep things the way they were. Terry was a good coordinator but he needed help with the bookkeeping.

RÉAL COUTU Cécile and I stayed friends. We actually would sometimes meet outside of board meetings and check in because sometimes it got too crazy. We called them 'les vraies réunions,' the real meetings. Things would get heated at those board meetings. We would touch base with each other to try and figure out priorities because sometimes in those meetings we covered so much. I would confess to Cécile! They were marathons and I often thought I agreed with something just to be able to go home. I don't know what VidPop board meetings are like now, but in our day every last thing was political.

LYDIA CARTWRIGHT I actually think that Carl-Yves's anxiety about women moving in and taking over is funny now but back then it made me absolutely livid. Let's just say he got yelled at a lot about his paranoia. Even Maurice, oblivious as he could be, shook his head when he heard that one about the women possibly 'encroaching.' Then Carl would turn on a dime and just love videos like Martha Rosler's *Semiotics of the Kitchen* and Doris Chase's *Electra Tries to Speak*. He freaked out over *Femmes de rêve* by Louise Gendron, which was like a critical barrage of advertising. There was a time there when Carl would insist that anyone who came to the centre had to watch those videos. I would actually come out and ask him which Carl I was addressing, the reactionary one who thought feminism was a secondary social issue, although he always denied that, or the guy who adored these key videos by women artists.

The camera thing was fucking unbelievable! I actually sat there and listened. And listened. We all did. I mean, it was laudable; we were trying to be respectful about purchasing a camera that was...in line with our Marxist ideals. Hours of debate. I think we bought a Sony in the end because we always bought Sony. And, really, no camera company was worse than any other.

Carl was not a constant pain in the ass or anything like that but he certainly had his moments. At first he was very righteous but after a few years of knowing him, you could look at him after one of his rants and say 'Are you quite finished, Carl?' and he would laugh.

CARL-YVES DUBÉ We could have built our own camera from parts. I'm sure of it. I'm pretty good with machines. Maurice was even better. He was all about precedents. He talked about the Lumière Brothers and Meliès as examples of people who built their own equipment. I think I reminded him those were film cameras and we were going to build a video camera. Very important difference. Maurice built some machines, signal attackers he called them, Moechines.

I would have tried. Then I don't even remember what kind of camera we did end up getting. One of the big names. Maurice and I would wait until everybody was gone and take apart one of Vidéo Populaire's cameras then put it back together. We were in training for building our own. I think we managed to keep our activities a secret. Except we almost got caught once. Maurice came in the next day and showed me this piece he had in his hand and he kept mouthing 'caméra.' I basically locked him in the edit suite so he could put the piece back before anyone else saw.

One thing that Maurice did for VidPop all the time he was there was care for and maintain equipment. He had no formal training but he was great at it. It was important because we didn't have much and what we did have needed to last.

ANTONIO DUTTO There were examples of people who were building their own machines. The big one I knew about was the Paik/Abe Synthesizer obviously. You have to remember, the editing of video in that first generation was expensive and time-consuming. And not always perfect, a bit hit or miss. Those homemade artist-made machines added so much to what you could do. I visited Montréal after they had bought their camera and Carl was kind of bitter that Maurice and he didn't have the support to build one themselves. But then Maurice also created his 'Moechines.' Those were awesome! The things you could do.

TERRENCE O'MEARA   We didn't formalize titles or job descriptions until the eighties. Oh, one of the things that bugged Carl-Yves and even Maurice was this idea that we were adopting corporate models of employment...When arts funding became more formal and more permanent, as in VidPop received money for operating, obviously there were things we needed to do. I couldn't just write 'we will take some swell videos on the road and show them to grateful people.' The early days were ours in a way, they belonged to us because we could do as we wished. We had no funding. We were all volunteering. For sure when you get funding you have to be accountable.

We almost always had a distribution coordinator after 1980. Lydia was the first. No, the second. But it was her idea originally. It wasn't just our own videos, we were taking videos by other artists, mostly Québécois and Canadian but some American and European. In the beginning the four of us did everything. Later on we had one position for each sector. Production Coordinator, Distribution Coordinator, Exhibitions Coordinator and Coordinator General. And part-time staff throughout the year to help with projects. Those titles were the least offensive — 'coordinator' was a good fit. We rejected 'director' and 'manager' as too corporate.

Working at a place like VidPop is a kind of vocation. I mean, you aren't doing it for money or glory.

MAURICE AUBERT   I couldn't sit still much unless I was tinkering with something. I sat most meetings out. Terry and Lydia understood, I think. But sometimes Terry would sit me down at the meeting table with something that needed repairing or cleaning. I didn't know what to say. I couldn't stay focused. I didn't understand what was going on with me. Working in the edit suite was the best thing. And repairing things. It kept a lot of bad things away from me. If I had stayed there with them I wonder if I might have avoided some bad times.

I had to learn something. And sometimes I don't think I've learned it at all. I had to learn to sit with the bad feelings. You kind of watch them without watching them. You kind of look around and notice them. Oh, hi. It's a whole technique. I don't know how many books I've read on the subject. I always think I'm doing it wrong. If I do it regularly, I do okay. If I get lazy, I get that seeping grey feeling.

CARL-YVES DUBÉ The fact that Maurice was slowly checking out kind of accelerated me checking out, too. To be honest, I didn't know what that meant then. I didn't know he and I were going. I tried to understand what Maurice was saying to me about feeling metallic, feeling a silver thing. I was out of my depth. Irritated, too. What the fuck was he talking about? How could he fall apart as we were gearing up for the next phase of our big project? That, I regret.

We started out doing everything. Outreach. Mobilizing. Producing. Going to meet workers and activists. We talked and talked about videos we wanted to make together. After five years it seemed like Maurice could only manage to do one thing. No. Two things: repairing machines and making his own work. Okay, three things. He could also make my work better. I've had years to think about this. I thought Vidéo Populaire would save us. Me. How fucking ridiculous. In some ways it did but not in all ways. I don't think Terrence and Lydia needed that. It was me and Maurice. Then I started thinking that Maurice would be saved if I left. It made me feel noble.

LYDIA CARTWRIGHT I had an okay family. My parents were decent. My brothers were good guys. But they didn't know what to make of me. There was always a gulf. I felt like I needed to explain myself to them but the older I got the less I wanted to. Get me, don't get me. It took the pressure off.

It was my first experience of belonging to something. I'd always been kind of on the outside, not quite a loner but not part of any clubs or cliques. It was the same for the others. That's why it was so hard to go.

MAURICE AUBERT It was hard for my family to understand what we were doing. When there started to be books about video art I would bring them to my parents to try and show them a little bit. It was obvious that I couldn't be a business-man unless the world flipped over completely and everything ran backwards and upside down. I started drawing when I was young and I just did it all the time. In school, in church, at dinner, all the time. That's how it has worked out for me. I do something all the time. I think I saw it in Carl before he saw it in me, that same thing. I want to say drive but I don't think that is exactly what I have. It's something, though, a kind of way of going and only stopping when you're sure it's okay.

TERRENCE O'MEARA I'll give you an example of the kinds of reactions Maurice's work could get. A curator wanted to do a retrospective of Vidéo Populaire's works. His name was Stephen Neil...Neil Stephen? No, Stephen Neil. He had been in the audience at a screening in Guelph where I showed Moe's work. I suspected what he really wanted to do was show all of Maurice's work but was too polite to say so. He came to VidPop often over a two-month period. He asked me for guidance about certain works. I showed him most of our stuff. I showed Stephen Carl-Yves's documentaries that were heavily influenced by Eisenstein and his ideas about montage. They were good, maybe a bit dated, but I loved them. Lydia did a whole series of performance-based feminist works. They were good, too, but Lydia is ambivalent about them now. I thought they still popped. I had a few of my own, too, but couldn't bring myself to look at them.

When Stephen got to Moe's work, I told him about the reactions that people tended to have. He told me he remembered me saying that by way of introduction at the Guelph screening but that he couldn't recollect having felt anything beyond interest. Hope grew in me. I hated myself. Moe's works were these eerie ruminations, abstract, intense. It was like they managed to get in and root around in each spectator's memories. I was hopeful that Stephen wouldn't succumb, that his retrospective would really end up being about all of VidPop, not just Moe.

When I came in the next day, there were five phone messages from Stephen.

'Hey, this is Stephen Neil for Terry. Terry, please call me when you get this.'

'Hi again, this is Stephen again for Terry. Terry...I'm sure you won't pick up your messages before tomorrow morning, but if you do, please call me when you can. It's 11:15.'

'Okay, Terry, you aren't gonna call me back tonight. I'm pretty sure of that and it's okay. I've been thinking...okay, I'll talk to you tomorrow.'

'I can't sleep. Terry. My heart is racing. I think I'm having one of those reactions maybe to Maurice's videos. Could that be? Days and weeks after I watched them? Have you ever heard of that? Okay....Okay...'

'Terry. Terry. It's impossible.'

Another Maurice Aubert retrospective coming up, I thought. I tried calling Stephen. There was no answer. In any case, he was supposed to arrive at 11:00 for more viewing.

He didn't show up.

I stayed late to finish up a grant. I wasn't very inspired. The trick for me was to write a little bit at a time no matter how awful I think it was. When I was younger I used to write grants in one sitting. On paper using a pen. I got slower and the technology got faster, thankfully.

The phone rang at 9PM. One ring. No one there. 'Stephen?' I asked into the receiver to no one. I hung up. The phone rang again about twenty minutes later. I snatched it up and said 'Hello Stephen — I know it's you. I'm here if you want to drop by. Okay? Or do you want to talk on the phone?'

'Yes.' It was Stephen. He hung up. I went back to my grant. Sometime around 10:30, I thought I heard something. It wasn't a knock, though. It was more like scratching. I went to the door and flipped the lock. Stephen was standing in the hallway several feet away. 'Stephen. I almost didn't hear you.'

'It's like I forgot how to knock. I think I ran my fingernails down the door even though I knew it wouldn't be very loud.'

'What's going on?' I asked.

'I was fine. I thought you planted those people at the screening. I really did. The woman called out something. Can't remember. And that guy who just stood up and wouldn't sit down. I thought they were in on it.'

'No. All that is Moe, or at least his videos.'

Yeah. Okay. Well I spent the night in the emergency ward. My heart just wouldn't stop racing. I tried to relax, breathe. Told myself it would pass. I've never had an anxiety attack before, but I feel like I'm having them all the time now. I've got to figure this out. What is this? I have a prescription for Ativan now. Ativan! I only used to take it recreationally....'

His arms were at his sides, rigid.

I told him something like 'I don't get anxious when I watch his work. I remember things that I have forgotten. It's different for everyone. That's how it works for me.'

'What am I gonna do? I don't feel well. And I don't want to show his work to other people. What happens if everyone has a bad reaction?'

'Come on in, Stephen, I'll make you some tea and we'll talk.'

'Will I make it?'

'Yes, of course you will.'

'I mean will I make it over there, to the door. I'm afraid I'm going to fall.'

Maurice the alchemist, I thought. I went over to Stephen and put out my arm like I was inviting a woman to dance. The party scene from *The Magnificent Ambersons* came to mind. He grabbed it and I led him to the door. 'You see, you did it. That was all you, I just put out my arm. You'll be fine.'

He was grinning now. 'Do you think this will go away if I never watch his work again?'

'Yes, I do.' I had no idea whether this was true or not. 'It's different for everyone who watches. As far as I can tell, some have no reaction during or after viewing.' I had hoped that Stephen would not concentrate only on Moe's troubling videos. Because I had hoped it, I now felt I had to fight for Moe. 'You know, it may seem hard for you right now, but you may come out of this with...something more.'

'Huh. You think so? Like, this is a bad patch before, I don't know, I have an epiphany or something?'

'Could be. I can't predict. I think Maurice's work deserves to be seen by...well, by as many people as possible.'

He wasn't holding on to me anymore. We moved into VidPop. I shut and locked the door. We walked to the back where the desks were and I offered him tea again.

'No, just water. No caffeine. Hey, I walked on my own there.'

'Yup. All you.' Stephen seemed to settle, his shoulders dropping down a bit.

'Yesterday, it was all him. I watched every video you gave me. And I liked most of them, too, loved some of them. But his. Well, you know. I had decided it was going to be a program with just his works. I was trying to figure out a way to tell you. That I would show his work and maybe in the future, would show yours and a few of Carl-Yves and Lydia's. I was thinking about titles. And about the text I would write. And words sort of began coming at me from, I don't know, a very far place. Zooming at me from the horizon. It was kind of fun at first. Zooming, like a low flying plane. At first I could make out the words. Then, not at all, and then I had to duck! I was actually ducking from words that were appearing from where? Then they changed direction and were kind of attacking me from behind. Attacking. I was dodging letters formed into words. I actually yelled 'stop!' And it did. It did. But nothing else did. The heart racing. The words, too, they would appear before my eyes but I couldn't make them out, oh maybe some of them, AWESOME, have you ever read the word 'awesome' in a serious text about videos? GRANDIOSE. Oh Jesus. Not even words I ever use. I thought that they were being sent by, I don't know, his videos? The signals, like, of his videos? I spent the worst twenty minutes of my life thinking I was unhinged. My girlfriend came over then and I freaked her out because I was sure she was going to be hit with a word. You know which word? BLISS. Now I can see that's it, it will have to appear in the title of the program. She thought I was completely drunk. I scared her and she left. She kept telling me to stop. I took myself off to the hospital. I knew I wouldn't be sharing any of this with a nurse or doctor. No flying words for them. Just anxiety. You get it, though, don't you? You've seen this or worse?'

'Not going to lie to you, Stephen. The flying words are new. But you aren't crazy. Clearly.'

'Yeah. Yeah. Except I don't want to watch those videos again. I just can't. And I should. I should watch them often to write about them. But I'm gonna have to rely on having seen them to put my text together. I know this is unusual, but I want to run something by you...Would you be okay with me asking you about the videos? Since you have seen them all so often?'

'Well, it's just like I told you before. Everybody reacts differently. Maybe even sees different things. I might only be able to tell you about my experiences, what I see.'

'Maybe I could write a story about that, about different reactions...gather up some info from spectators and do it that way...Where are the videos now?'

He suddenly looked like the poor guy in *An Occurrence at Owl Creek Bridge*.

'What?'

'Where are the tapes you showed me the other day?'

'Back on the shelves there.'

'Where?'

I pointed to the shelves behind him. Stephen spun around in his chair.

This was a new one, too. Someone was frightened by the proximity of the objects. 'Stephen, I don't feel comfortable with your proposal. I can provide you with info on all the work, but I don't want my ideas on his work to...to be the backbone of your text.'

'Could you move them, please?'

'Pardon?'

'Move his tapes, please.' I got up and went to the shelves, pulling down Moe's videos. I walked with them to the smaller edit suite, put them on a table and shut the door. 'It was starting to happen again, the word thing, and they were coming from the shelves. See, it's stopped now.'

I had seen enough weird stuff around those videos.

Stephen stood up. 'No, I won't be able to watch them again. I don't think I can even be in the same room with them. I'm going now. I'll call you.' He hesitated. I walked over to him and put my arm out. He gripped it and I walked him to the door, flipped the lock, and we continued through the lobby to the street.

'Do you want me to call you a taxi?'

'I want to say yes. But I feel like I should try walking home on my own. If I can't do that, I don't know.' I watched him go. He sort of shuffled, sliding his feet along the sidewalk. He called out something but I couldn't hear so I went up to him. 'What do you think the Moechines actually do?'

'They alter the video signal.'

'Are you sure that's all they do?'

I went back inside and was suddenly furious with Moe. I opened the door to the edit suite and looked at the stack of his videos. I stared at them for a long while, willing words to come at me. I was jealous of Stephen Neil and his experience. If he wrote it right, his could be a very original and funny text. He could explain what had happened to him and readers would just think he was making a point about the visceral nature of Maurice's videos. A clever way into the work. It would help, I thought, if Moe would talk about his work. Even a bit. I looked at the two old monitors sitting on the shelves, dark and knowing. They had looked so sleek and modern when we bought them. I decided to take one over to Moe's and leave it at his doorstep. I would knock and go.

I couldn't write any more. I took the monitor off the shelf. It was heavy and covered in dust. Moe was right. I was just displaying the old technology. It wasn't serving a purpose. I locked up VidPop and cradled the monitor in my arms all the way to Coloniale. I went up the stairs, put the monitor down and knocked once. I didn't linger. I just turned around, went down the stairs and walked home. I never saw Stephen Neil again.

An order came in for all of Maurice's videos. I received five copies of a pamphlet with a text by Stephen Neil. The photograph of Maurice was one I took of him in 1979. Impossibly young with that shoulder-length hair. The image was cropped. What people don't see is that he is holding one of his popcorn sandwiches just below the frame. The photo is the only one anyone ever uses.

NANCY AMIOT   Those legendary reactions to Maurice Aubert's work! I've seen his videos many times. I'm writing a paper about the seventies and the Québec video scene right now. About ten years back I watched his work for the first time and then I had a kind of mild shift in my eyesight. I thought, 'Could it be?' Turns out I couldn't blame Maurice, because I just got my first floaters, you know, in the eye. I've never had anything like the intense reactions described by Terrence. I will say though that his work has an effect on me. I find I can only watch one video in a sitting and if it is a longer piece like *No 5*, I have to take a break.

GUILLAUME R. BOIVIN   The four of them were insular. I didn't get the sense that you could be part of it, VidPop, but later on it seemed to open up a bit, probably because the two oddballs abandoned ship. I was much more affected by Carl-Yves's work. Everybody was all about Maurice, even now, but not me. It's kind of like an urban legend.

SERGE MASSON   I watched Maurice and Carl-Yves edit. I had it in my mind that I wanted to learn to do that, too. They had completely different ways of working. Sometimes Maurice would sit and stare at an image for a really long time. If Carl was there, it would drive him crazy and he would try to prod Maurice into doing something. I was kind of on Carl's side with that.

Back when Carl thought I was still worth having around, Maurice asked me to watch a rough cut of one of his videos. I can't even tell you what happened. I went in the room to watch. And I came out an hour later but it's like I lost time. Maurice kept asking me what I thought, should he change this or that? Was this too much? I didn't know. I thought maybe someone had put something in whatever I was drinking. It wasn't unheard of to add a little something to your drink. There was a smell, too, like bread baking, only sharper. The farther that memory gets the less sure I am of any of it.

DAVID SUMMERVILLE   Oh, fabulous, fabulous stories! I wish I had come up with some of them myself. Terry would tell me things in his serious Terry voice and I would say 'Now, Terry, the seventies have left the building definitively.'

ROSEMARY DRUMMOND   Nothing. You would think I was a prime candidate, being all chakra-centric and everything else. Nada.

LYDIA CARTWRIGHT   Is it something Terry and Maurice cooked up together? Terry suggests how about if I go around planting people in the audience? How about if I tell stories about how people have reacted to the work? The power of suggestion. I think I would have known if something like that was going on. Terry is so not a vault; he can't keep secrets.

I have my own story about his videos anyways. I was at VidPop late. Maurice had been in the edit suite forever as usual. I'd been hearing this one section he was working on over and over. We had a fairly big space back then, but what we called the 'edit suite' was really just a big room with no sound insulation. It had a door. The repetition of the same sequence was kind of making me loopy. You know what, I dream of that exact section once in a while. I only hear the audio, like I did that time. I don't see images, even though I know that tape very well. I can't be sure, but it's like I see just black then hear the words. It's from Maurice's *No 10*. 'Oh misère, oh câlisse, oh, oh baptême, oh, hé Guy hé attends-moé.' Exactly those words. It was this random bit of dialogue by a passing guy that Maurice got when he was shooting on the street. So when I hear those other stories I guess I'm willing to believe them somehow.

CÉCILE GRONDIN I always thought it was an in-joke. Those guys were so different from each other but, I don't know, there was something between Terry and Maurice that suggested they might have invented those things. Terry has a sneaky sense of humour. Maurice, too. Unpredictable. But Terry is one of the most honest guys I've ever known. For me, Maurice's work is something that stays on the screen, it doesn't reach out and do things to me.

LUISA SEPÚLVEDA I've had conversations with Maurice about emanations, ghosts, *revenants* and other things over the years. What I can say is that he, Maurice, feels things about other people's work very strongly. He would talk about how videos and films affected him. For me, I'm open, I can believe some of the stories. Maurice would ask me about that shot in our film, *Spiritos*, the one where I walk towards the camera. He would ask 'what were you thinking?' I didn't remember and I didn't want to lie to him. But he is someone who thinks about those things constantly, feels them.

MAURICE AUBERT   Terry used to tell me about odd reactions to my work, but I asked him to stop. I don't think I've ever watched anything I made with an audience. When I used to go to screenings a long time ago I waited outside. At first it was flattering I guess. Then I started to feel that maybe I'd unleashed something terrible. Terry and I went to see *The Exorcist* when it came out. I regret it to this day. I had to sleep with the lights on for months. I started thinking along those lines...that my own work might be releasing something. And then later on *Ringu* came out. If you watched a video, you would die. Video kills. I don't believe that. But I kind of think something might be caught in tape. That began a long period for me. I didn't want to research demons but I did and I couldn't stop. Sulak is the ancient demon of latrines...There are lots of demons and some of them are in charge of the smallest things.

I wish Terry didn't get these sudden urges to move things or clean up. When Terry walked towards me with a 3/4" tape in his hand, I got a terrible feeling. I didn't know it came from Carl's box but I kind of did, too. It doesn't matter what's on that video. I don't know. I doubt Carl would have left something important behind. He left so angry. I can't imagine holding that videotape in my hands. I just feel like tape has its own orbit and gravity. Some can pull you in.

I went through a time where I thought it would be best to pull my videos. Never have them shown again. I might have believed that some of me, the bad part, was getting transferred into my work. I never loved my tapes the way Terry does. I mean, I do like them generally but he carries them. It's Carl's videos that make me see things.

ELSA SMITH   I saw Maurice's videos often when I worked for VidPop doing a video tour of Montréal. I loved his work but I have nothing special to report, I'm sorry to say. During the screenings people would sometimes get up and leave but that isn't uncommon. I kind of wanted something to happen. Maybe I wanted it too much. There was this story going around that you had to be in a kind of neutral state to experience something. I never was in neutral because I was always thinking about the questions after the screening, how to get the ball rolling.

RÉAL COUTU I'll tell you what I've told Terry many times. When I quit the chicken delivery, I didn't have any work. I basically quit because I wanted to do something new. It seemed that everybody around me was actually working at something they liked and I wanted that, too. I moved to this small one-bedroom place to cut costs. It was really badly insulated and freezing cold. I got sick. So the story about me shaking at a screening of Aubert's work can be explained. I was sick! Terry has a tendency to embellish. He saw me shivering and there you have it, more evidence of this 'Moe Effect.'

ANTONIO DUTTO Carl never ever believed any of those things about Maurice's work. He is my main contact so I have kind of gone along with him. Great stories, though. But then I've met Terry and spent time with him and I just don't get that from him that he would make those kinds of things up. Maurice is unique for sure. Seeing him work was kind of shamanistic. Oh, man.

But I have a story that is not quite about Maurice's videos. It's more about Maurice's insight. When I was back home I started on my project with and about my brother Joe. Joe got drafted and went over to Nam in 69 at age twenty-two. He did two tours. It ruined him in some way that no one got at first. I wanted to make a video about this regular guy who became this anti-war activist. He built himself back up into someone, those are his own words, over the years after he had been kind of destroyed. The point of this is that before I left Montréal I talked to Maurice about how to begin the project. I had these ideas about one shot or another but I wasn't sure. Something was stopping me. I really respected Maurice and his work. He never said much. He told me to let Joe figure out the first shot.

ROGER CROSS Terry felt that it was part of his job as coordinator to fill new staff in on what he called 'The Moe Effect.' It was almost like part of the job training. I never experienced anything weird myself and I saw those videos often, making copies, checking them. The only thing and it really isn't much is that I always seemed to see a new image in a work I knew really well. I've always thought the stories were an eccentric VidPop thing, like stuff was just so freaky in the seventies and this was the kind of work you produced.

NORMAND CÔTÉ A video is just a fucking video! Come on, Terry should get some kind of an award for coming up with that shit. I think some of Aubert's work is great. But really. You don't hear or see or smell anything.

LORENZO SEPÚLVEDA There are enough ghosts, no need to go looking for more. I like it, though, a mystical approach to art. For me, it isn't his videos, it's Maurice himself. Some people are like sponges and some can shut their steel doors before you know it, bang! Maurice is a sponge. He picks up on everything.

I have watched videos and films with Maurice regularly. He invites me over and we choose from his collection of work. There is often a moment where Maurice will say 'there, right there, look' like he is trying to point out something that I might miss.

CARL-YVES DUBÉ I never had a surprising reaction to his videos. I just hated that stuff back then, thought it was unnecessary, the wrong way to go. It meant so much to me that we were trying to shift things politically. When Maurice went all out experimental, I despised it. I don't know what to say. I said the things I said and felt the way I felt. And then I didn't. I'm happy for him. That his work is so respected.

When Maurice saw that film *Arnulf Rainer* by Peter Kubelka, he almost packed it all in. Maurice told me he thought that was it, it has all been said, forget it. I tried to reason with him but for a while I thought he was done. *Arnulf Rainer*. This is a bad description, but the film is made up of alternating black and white leader. The sound is off or on, it alternates, too. What's the sound...I don't recall. I only saw it once. That's what I saw. What there was to see, I saw. Maurice saw images between the black and white leader. They aren't there. At least not for me.

Watching Maurice work was something. I had my own process which, you can imagine, was very different. And my way was probably very much like other directors. I would think about segments and organize footage thematically. Maurice just dug in and free-associated. Process. I was more about product.

Him and me, we both really liked Arthur Lipsett's work. We agreed on some artists, quite a few even. You can see the influence Lipsett had on Maurice.

TERRENCE O'MEARA I know what I've seen. I know what I've felt myself.

I have a fantasy that Maurice will make a new video for the 40th anniversary screening. His images and sounds would do their thing, spill out over the room, and we'd have proof at last. Because the room would be packed with artists, curators, representatives from arts funders and government officials. Then everybody would get it. Get what, exactly? That's just it — I don't know. Whatever it is.

I have had a few theories about Moe's videos over the years. Currently, I'm going with this idea that his videos are quite restrained in a sense. They don't lead you to a foregone conclusion. There is space for people to let their minds wander. After a time, I think 'Terry, just stop.' Because there is no explanation. Maurice talks about ghosts sometimes. He always has a pet, a cat or a dog, sometimes both. He had this cat named Shark once. That cat was sweet and smart. Maurice really loved him. Found him on the street and took him home. When Shark died, Maurice went to pieces. I went to stay with him off and on for a few weeks. That tells you a lot right there. I would just show up, the door would be unlocked and I would go in and sleep on his couch. Just to be there. He told me that he could feel Shark's presence. I suppose I told him that was normal, that you felt he was still in the apartment. No, he said, you'll see. Maurice made *No 19* that year. It was about Shark. Without being about Shark. I've seen it dozens of times. Each time I watch it, I still think there will be images of that cat in the video. There aren't any. Not a mention either. Maybe the idea of alchemy or osmosis is too strong. Maybe I've been too close to these videos over the years.

I get migraines. I've had them since I was about fourteen. I don't know how many people have told me that's it, that's the answer, my migraines have caused me to see things in Maurice's videos. My question is this: does everyone who has experienced something suffer from migraines?

NANCY AMIOT I wanted to talk to Maurice about his work, his process, how he made videos. I wanted to ask about the equipment he actually made to play with the video signal. I first talked to Terry, who gave me Maurice's address and phone number and also some advice. He told me that Maurice was not much for talking and that a more formal approach was in order. I wanted to try. I wrote him a letter, introducing myself and telling him that I'd been spending a lot of time at Vidéo Populaire researching and working on programs. Terry wrote him a letter. I called. The phone just rang and rang. Nothing. Terry actually accepted to bring me over to Maurice's place and introduce me if he answered the door. We did that but I never met him.

I eventually got a note, a three-word response in the mail from Maurice: *Watch my videos*. At first I was irritated. No kidding. I felt like writing back 'what do you think I've been doing?' I showed it to Terry and he laughed and nodded. But that's the key, isn't it? Watch his videos. He will never confirm this, but I think he means that each viewer will see what needs to be seen.

I think several curators have had to change the focus of their texts because Maurice Aubert won't ever comment on his work.

MARIE CHEVRIER   I started going out with Maurice because of his videos. They blew me away. That's all they did. I didn't see or hear anything that wasn't already in his videos. Maurice kind of had groupies. He didn't encourage it. I think it actually scared him.

He was, is, a sweet, sweet guy but not good boyfriend material. I was only on the periphery of Vidéo Populaire. Maurice and I went out for maybe two years. If I wanted to see him, I pretty much had to go to VidPop. I didn't mind at first but then it dawned on me that I was making every decision about 'us.' Maurice was just into his work. That's all. It wasn't dramatic. I stayed friends with him, Lydia and Terry. I thought Carl-Yves was okay, really. While Maurice and I were together, he was good to Maurice. And they were close, I thought.

ELSA SMITH I got the job by talking to Terrence at an event. I had done some publicity work for a small film festival and had facilitated workshops. The first contract was for three months. I probably was there a bit longer, though. The second contract was for a bit longer.

I was hired to take a program of videos around Montréal to different places: community groups, youth centres. The idea was to take video to people who were unlikely to come to screenings at VidPop or art galleries. Often one or more of the video artists would accompany me. I would intro the screening, present the directors. We would watch the program and there would be questions afterwards.

We had to bring the equipment! In those days, it was almost unheard of for little organizations to have any way of showing videos. Everything was so heavy, the monitor and the player. I couldn't have done it on my own.

We made photocopies of the program that we passed out at screenings.

The 'I' in me, Lydia Cartwright, 1980, 6 minutes
Le travail, Carl-Yves Dubé, 1979, 45 minutes
No 7, Maurice Aubert, 1978, 11 minutes

Lydia was almost always able to connect with the audience. She was a good public speaker and took questions well, because sometimes the questions were difficult. Not everybody was open to experimental work. In some of the places we went, some people almost took it personally, like, what are you trying to put over on us?

I may be one of the rare people who actually stood in the same room as Maurice Aubert prior to one of his videos showing. Maurice came along maybe once, maybe twice. He wouldn't say a word. I tried. When his video showed, he would leave the room. If Carl-Yves was there, he would go outside with him. They would roll cigarettes and have a smoke, thick as thieves.

Carl-Yves was always ready for a debate. His work *Le travail* was strong. The days of thinking that video represented a kind of utopia were just about waning. This was the early eighties. We were trying to turn people onto independent video one viewer at a time. Looking back, I'm not sure we picked up that many converts, but I loved that project. I loved watching those videos in different settings all around Montréal. Church basements, community centres, meeting halls of all kinds.

DR. TIMOTHY PETERSON Carl convinced me to install a monitor with a VCR in my waiting room. And I did it. He was very persuasive as I'm sure you have experienced. I said to him I didn't want any of those videos about people eating broken light bulbs or cutting themselves with knives. I didn't want to see Lydia eating videotape. I heard about what Maurice's videos were supposed to be able to do to people. I didn't completely believe it but I didn't want to take a chance. From Maurice you could believe such things. Carl selected some videos to show me first and they were good, I liked them, and I said yes. I showed them like I said

I would. Carl explained to me about artist fees and I paid VidPop for the rental of the videos. We did that for a few years. Like I said, I learned a lot. It was a whole other world than mine. I liked not doing exactly what was expected of me. You know, quite a few members of VidPop became my patients and they also told other people, who liked this idea that I was a little out there.

Terry asked me if I would be willing to reprise the experience of showing videos in my waiting room for the 40th anniversary and I said yes. We would show the same works from back then and some newer videos.

MAURICE AUBERT I started out strong and part of something. By the time Marie figured out who I was, I had figured it out, too.

Each one of them backed me. Terry, Lydia, Carl. Pierre. Antonio. Dr. Tim. Some others. Danielle, of course. Rosemary. Marcel. Laurent. Luisa. They took me on. I couldn't explain myself to people anymore and Carl told me I didn't have to. That isn't the last thing he said to me but it is the main thing.

I did go back. To VidPop. Three times. I kept the keys and let myself in. I would have done it more often but I had trouble getting there. At night. It was easier for me to move at night because I saw less of the things that bothered me. I didn't tell Terry or Lydia. I figured they would know because I have an imprint like everyone else, a presence. I'm sure I felt Carl-Yves one of the times. I would sit and look out the window onto the street. I would sit with the machines and tapes. Sometimes I would tinker with some of the machines. I would walk around and look at the posters. VidPop had a particular smell, a good one. Not quite the smell of printing, like ink on paper, or orange peels, but something kind of in between mixed with the smell of tapes. There was also a bakery nearby on St-Laurent and if the wind was right, that smell would get folded in, too.

CARL-YVES DUBÉ I went back once in 1984. Only Lorenzo knew. After months of thinking about it, I went over at 4 AM.

I asked Lorenzo for information on comings and goings so I wouldn't run into anyone. And I asked to borrow his keys to the new space. When I'd left, I didn't know I was leaving for good. I felt like I wanted to look at the space. I didn't know what I wanted at all, but I went. If Terrence had seen me, he would have listed a series of film references because I was dressed all in black, including a watch cap on my head, like a burglar.

I was happy to see the posters. The space smelled good. I think I just stood there for some time. If I had sat and slept and was still there the next morning, would it have been so bad? I think we would have just gone on, continued, they would have seen me and we would have talked, maybe argued a bit. I didn't sit.

LYDIA CARTWRIGHT It was tough when Carl-Yves left. I was so angry with him. Was there a broken window that time? I think there was a broken or cracked window. Bang. Then nothing. VidPop became very quiet when Carl left. And Maurice. His leaving was sad. He just sort of ebbed. I believe we let him down. There was a gap of four years, give or take, between Carl and Maurice leaving but I always have to remind myself of that.

Towards the end of Carl's involvement, I felt like I needed some kind of universal translator or interpreter. Carl would say something like 'The sun is setting.' And the sun *would* be setting but I think he meant way, way more than that. I thought he was speaking Marxist. It could have been funny if I'd had anyone to share it with but we were all a little in our own spaces then. I started to suspect that Carl and Maurice were using albums to talk at each other. Maurice brought in *Los Angeles* by X. Carl played *Uprising* by Bob Marley & The Wailers. They would crank up the volume. I actually thought I would also bring in a record, something they both really hated. I would play it and it would unite them against me.

My interest in VidPop started to flag. There we were, Terry and I. I don't even really know what Terry thinks about that time now. We spent most of our energy holding on. I thought we couldn't do it without the other two. Those two, the ones who left, were extreme in different ways and Terry and I together were so agreeable. I think I was worried we would just stay the course and somehow sink VidPop because we weren't extreme enough, didn't push enough. I'm not explaining this well, but I felt like we were lopsided without Carl-Yves and Maurice.

I don't mean to say we were alone at VidPop. We weren't, but it was quite strange. I thought seriously of going, too. In the eighties, I kind of experienced this renewed commitment. I thought often of Carl, who had been so blown away by those videos he'd seen in New York in the seventies. I went to New York in...oh probably 1988 and saw a screening of HIV/AIDS activist videos. They were made the way we always thought videos should be made, from the inside. I brought some titles back to Montréal to suggest that VidPop distribute them. I stayed for two more years.

WILLIAM JARDIN Montréal was not New York. But I knew guys who were sick. I learned that this place Vidéo Populaire was having a screening of videos about HIV. I went with a friend, Michel (Robitaille), and we met Lydia and Terrence. I didn't know a thing about what they did there. There were all these flyers lying around that described the services they offered. Michel and I talked to Lydia because she had brought these videos up from New York and she introduced them. We ended up talking about making a documentary on the situation in Montréal, the services, the resources. It was us suggesting to her and we didn't expect to be involved but we ended up co-directing it, the three of us. I didn't have any experience. I kind of went to school, going there to watch videos by GMHC, Testing the Limits and others. Oh, yes, *Bright Eyes* by Stuart Marshall. *DHPG, mon amour*. Those tapes and films where you could feel the activism in a way.

LYDIA CARTWRIGHT William wanted to start the video with the way HIV had been identified in the beginning, Gay Cancer, GRID (Gay Related Immune Deficiency), and the idea of blame. There was a whole narrative of blame then. Then. Has it ever quite gone away? Finding the original 'AIDS carrier' wasn't a desirable or useful exercise. Like finding out would solve anything. Telling people how to be safe was the focus. Telling them about resources. So we embarked on that. It was a long process. We so wanted to get it right. I think we tried to get so much into that video that we eventually had to cut back. The rough cut was something like ninety-eight minutes. Our goal was to get it to fifty. We got it to sixty. Michel was HIV-positive and was starting to have some health problems. He suggested we interview him about his experiences. 'Who better?' he said.

WILLIAM JARDIN Michel was seeing an herbologist and also having acupuncture treatments. He would say, 'I'm famous, look, there's a camera crew following me everywhere.' And, yes, we really were following him quite a bit. Michel was always making snide remarks because he had never believed in what he called the granola new age crap and there he was going to all these practioners. Lydia showed Michel and I how to work the camera. Later on, Terry and Lydia gave us workshops in editing. Michel didn't have the longest attention span and would just tell story after story about this guy or that guy or this sexy weekend in the country. Terry would try to get Michel to concentrate by showing us different things we could do in the editing. It was a funny mix, all of us together. I used to love watching Terry's attempts to get Michel to make even one editing decision.

I taped Michel at his apartment, him bouncing all over the place, talking about his day, his appointments, work, guys, his aunt who became kind of his mother when his real mother couldn't accept a gay son. It took us over a year to shoot and edit. While we made *Positive* Michel quit smoking and drinking and drugs. He cut out red meat. He had to give away his two cats. Siamese. I offered to take one but they had to remain together. It broke his heart.

NANCY AMIOT *Positive Montréal* is also kind of a snapshot of Montréal in the late eighties. There are images of demonstrations, critiques of government information and safe-sex campaigns, interviews with people in the street. It is very vibrant, full of information. The segments with Michel Robitaille give a look at what it was like before the *trithérapie*, the cocktail.

One of the criticisms that HIV/AIDS activists had was that government safe-sex campaigns were always too general. Even worse, sometimes the ads were threatening, almost like horror films. Ever seen the 'death goes bowling' Public Service Announcement?

LYDIA CARTWRIGHT Michel and William did their research and then some. They even taped a segment where they sat, talk-show style, and bashed different government safe-sex campaigns. We had some disagreements about that only because the segment was so long and they wanted to keep it all. Michel died in 1993. By then I had left VidPop. William called to tell me. We asked Terry if we could hold a memorial screening of *Positive* at VidPop. Robert T. Roberts came to the screening and thanked William and Michel for initiating the production program.

WILLIAM JARDIN I don't know how many times I've introduced *Positive* and shown it to audiences over the years. It doesn't get shown as much anymore, of course, but there has been a mini-revival. It used to be hard but now it's good to see Michel and hear his voice. I asked Lydia to speak the night we did the screening for Michel, because I was too broken up. I just stood there beside her. Michel's aunt Huguette came. It was so touching, this smartly dressed woman of about seventy. It was good, too, because there are funny parts in that video and everyone laughed with Michel, especially Huguette.

TERRENCE O'MEARA After finishing *Positive*, William and Michel came up with a proposal for VidPop to have a program to co-produce HIV/AIDS activism videos. Lydia was on her way out but she really lobbied for that. Once a year, artists could apply for access to equipment, including editing. Sometimes, people who did apply had other funding. Often not. In the nineties we helped produce seven or eight short videos. We still award a grant each year. William asked that we name it the Michel Robitaille Production Fund and everyone agreed. Last year, we helped produce webisodes made by, I think, fifteen people, most of them under twenty.

WILLIAM JARDIN I send people to Vidéo Populaire all the time. In the nineties I was on the committee for the Michel Fund to select the projects.

I'm trying to work on a new documentary, one that looks at the history of Montréal AIDS activism and services. I still call up Lydia for advice.

ROBERT T. ROBERTS At one point I didn't mind that people called me Bobby2. I even encouraged it. I like to think that my parents had no idea how tough it would be to have a name like the one they gave me. Anyhow, I added an initial for my middle name Thomas and I like to be called Robert now. Oh, someone had it worse than me. A guy called Guy Ostiguy. We met there, at VidPop. He was also working on a video. People called him 'Hostie de Guy' all the time.

DAVID SUMMERVILLE I joked about changing my name to David David. Went over like a lead balloon. I thought there must be some kind of weird video karma thing. All these people with crazy names were showing up at VidPop. There was a whole wave of gay guys with funny names in the nineties. Guy Ostiguy had enough at one point. He changed his name legally. I can only remember that he became Serge something.

ROBERT T. ROBERTS I really did have a dream in which I was talking with a friend of mine, James. He'd been dead quite a long time. I wrote down the main points of my dream and left it alone. I only dreamed it once as far as I know but it really stayed with me, probably because I rarely remember my dreams. Then I wrote it out again, more as a kind of text. I left it alone for a long while. Maybe I saw the Vidéo Populaire announcement somewhere on a bulletin board at school or an art gallery. There was a flyer about a production fund for making videos about issues related to HIV. I didn't think of my dream at first. I thought they were looking for non-fiction. But a professor of mine told me I should submit. I was using sections from my dream in my artwork, installations mostly.

This is the text I sent in with my application

I see something out of the corner of my eye.
A figure maybe. I don't know.

I don't know who you are. Do I say this out loud?
You are like the guys in *Cruising*.
You are like the guys in *Testing the Limits*.

The borders seem to be blue.
I didn't know there were borders but these happen to be blue
a clear blue I can see through
and you are clear now.
Your clearness is unbelievable.
I say it is you!

Yes, me.

I can't wait to wake up and share the news
but just thinking that
means I dream.

You are you in my dream.
Tell me something I say
before you go.

I have nowhere to go but I'll tell you this
My thumb hurts
I'll tell you this
I walk at night
I'll tell you this
tie your shoelaces
I'll tell you this
I listen to Patti Smith and Linda Ronstadt
In the elevator
I have forgotten myself

I say I want you back

Back like what?
Back like dust?
Back like gas?
Back like a clump of hair?
Back like pus?

Okay
I want to go back

Good luck to you
if you are going back
bring me something good from now
bring me an MP3 player
are they really better than walkmans?
load it up with Patti Smith
and bring me a Frappuccino
bring me whatever you can carry
think, too, think of good and smart things to bring
supplies and recipes and strategic plans
pills
don't just bring licorice and magazines
like you did when you visited me

You grow thinner and clearer

I also had a separate sheet where I had described some of the visuals. Looking back, my proposal was just terrible. But it got accepted. I got paired up with a mentor, a filmmaker named Ghislaine Bérubé, and took some camera and editing courses. Ghislaine and I maybe weren't the best fit but she had some great ideas and I respected her. She was trying to get me to shape the video into something...I think she said 'manageable.' She was kind of terrified or maybe disdainful that I had no real script. I also met with Luisa Sepúlveda when I was editing and she was encouraging. Lydia suggested I watch some of Maurice Aubert's and Carl-Yves's videos and others in the VidPop collection. That did it. Loved those works, felt that I wanted to emulate them. Guy Ostiguy and I were finishing our productions around the same time so we hung out a fair bit. I made *Dream One* in 1996-1997. It's short, five minutes, and most of the images are shot just outside VidPop in the hall which was very industrial looking. It's my only video.

MAURICE AUBERT I like many of those videos but I especially like that one about seeing a ghost. It has nice narration, just someone talking. Not a trained voice. I often don't like those trained voices. I can see what the outside of the new office looks like.

There is a sample from a song by Klaus Nomi in that video. Klaus Nomi...I heard about him while I was still at VidPop. We kept a record player there. It seems like every once in a while we would bring in music we were listening to at our places. Lydia brought in that first album, I think it was called 'Klaus Nomi.' Then he was gone. Oh, what did Carl bring in once...Jobriath.

NANCY AMIOT There has always been a misconception that Vidéo Populaire tapes are mostly documentary. I find that amazing, especially since Maurice and Lydia certainly participated in making some documentaries, but their individual works are anything but. Something like *Dream One* by Robert T. Roberts is a kind of conversation between a man and his dead friend. I'm going to pair it with *Positive Montréal* in a program. I actually just heard someone say, someone who should know better, that videos like *Dream One* are an anomaly in the collection. It's like they only know the videos from the seventies.

WILLIAM JARDIN   I fought for *Dream One*. I thought it was just so different from many of the proposals we got and that was good. At first, Michel and I hadn't known anything about making a video but we got help from VidPop and we figured it out. I don't think *Positive* is perfect or anything, but I think it did what needed to be done. I forget the name of one of the guys who was on the committee but he kept saying there was nothing to evaluate about *Dream One*, just some words.

SERGE DUVAL   My parents must have hated me from day one, giving me a name like Guy Ostiguy. The teasing and abuse started right away and never really stopped. I even got teased at Vidéo Populaire, but it was somehow different. It was more...light. When I became a member there to work on my documentaries, I met Robert. We shared similar name problems.

I knew I was gay by the time I was eight or nine. Knew it but didn't understand yet. My decision to change my name was partly to deny my parents the right to make jokes *plates* at my expense. There was one day when someone working at Vidéo Populaire called out 'Hostie de guy!' but there was no lightness to it. It wasn't one of the main people or the regulars. I decided then and there to pick a new name. I tried to convince Robert to do it, too. We bonded over our unfortunate names, initially. Then we started talking about our work. I watched him make *Dream One*. I don't think I could ever make a work like that. I admired it. I kind of drank it in. It was about things that were starting to happen to me and my friends.

DAVID SUMMERVILLE The thing I like best about VidPop are all the collaborations. That is something to celebrate and honour. A good example is the Michel Robitaille Fund helping with the production of videos made by local artists about HIV. And lots of other projects besides, where VidPop partnered with different centres to make a video. Women's centres, unions, food banks. Terry is always asked to tell the same stories. I like to tell different ones. I never thought William and Michel would ever come through with their video but they did. It was a good thing they had Lydia. I did a few things on the production. Michel would always show up late, I'm talking hours, or he would forget altogether. William was constantly covering for him. Lydia had to give them an ultimatum, the video had to be done by such-and-such a date because she was afraid it would just not get done at all. She didn't want to be in a position where she finished it herself, because she felt it was not her place. I remember seeing a rough cut that was over ninety minutes. And another that was about eighty. I said to them 'keep cutting' because there was some good stuff. So here is the important part. Lydia was out of town and she asked me to check in when Michel and William were editing. I go in and they are so sorry to see me, uncomfortable. I ask to see where they are at, to show me the cut. They had crammed some old and new stuff in there, pushing it over ninety minutes again. I gave them the less-is-sometimes-more speech. It didn't go well. They said I was a lapdog. They said it was their video. I told them 'Yes, it is YOUR video, so don't fuck it up.' Collaborations aren't always a piece of cake. We sorted it out when Lydia came back. We organized these kind of test screenings, their longer version and the version we thought worked better. We had different people, some who knew about the project and some who didn't. That's what did it. Michel and William got much better reactions over the shorter version. And Lydia and I didn't have to step in.

ROBERT T. ROBERTS I really, really wanted to meet Maurice. Someone, might have been Lydia, said 'join the club.' I also wanted to meet Carl-Yves and asked Terrence about that. 'Tell me how you get on,' he said. Of course, I never met either of them but I always hoped they saw *Dream One*. Guy, um Serge, and I had this elaborate plan to show up at Maurice's front door and convince him to watch our videos. Terry talked us out of it, but assured us that Maurice would see our work.

I just loved those stories about Maurice's videos and all that mystical shit. I was thinking about that a lot when I was editing.

TERRENCE O'MEARA I got depressed when Lydia left for good. She did it in stages and we talked about her leaving often but I still felt awful. I think I saved up my Carl-is-gone and Maurice-is-gone depressions and just experienced everything all at once. But it wasn't like the others. She didn't disappear like Carl-Yves. Maurice didn't vanish. I knew where he was but I couldn't always reach him. I could call her. She kept her distance for a while and then she felt it was okay to come back for events. We could always talk.

Board and staff members were floating around the idea of making a documentary about the history of Vidéo Populaire. After our 35th anniversary we started brainstorming for the 40th. I called up Lydia. She came to the office for a coffee and we talked about it for a few hours. Weeks later we talked again and we both said practically the same thing, that we are too close to the material. I wouldn't know where to begin even though everybody says I'm the VidPop guy. I'm the VidPop guy by default. Lydia is as much that guy as I am. We've been talking to some directors who we think could do a good job. I've been suggesting people who were around from that time, people who knew us. Lydia has a list of younger directors who she says would do lots of research. She also mentioned Antonio and I think that he would be perfect somehow. He would be perfect but I've talked to him and he would only consider doing it if he could get us all in a room. As far as I'm concerned, I would love that. Lydia too. It's Carl, really. I also wanted to add Bobby2 to the list, and William. Why limit it to people who knew early VidPop?

It doesn't feel right. Maurice knows. I've told him about the idea. I asked him if he would agree to be interviewed. 'And say what?' he said. To be expected. Then I asked him to select excerpts of some of his videos that could be included. He said, 'You're better at that stuff.' But with Carl-Yves, I feel sick about it. I want him to know, too, and decide yes or no. When it's taking shape, if it takes shape, I will try to contact him. Or try and convince Lydia to do it.

LYDIA CARTWRIGHT   I feel like we might screw it up somehow even though we are the ones who were there. What goes in? The napkin story? Maurice's popcorn fixation? Carl-Yves punching his way through the seventies? Terry and his film trivia? Gee, if I was to complete that equation, what would I reduce myself to? I have one video where I play solitaire half-naked. That would do.

Terry was pulling out names, people I barely remembered, who had something to do with VidPop at different points, and we both got overwhelmed. I've been thinking that we all might want to look at documentaries that talk about the truth being elusive. Or maybe this whole VidPop documentary idea would be better as a fiction film. It might be funny to summarize the first year with one of those cheesy movie montages they use to condense time. Bad upbeat music, shot of us meeting at the party. Shot of us laughing over coffee. Of course, this time the napkin would be the focus and it would make it into my bag. Next shot arguing around a table. Searching for an office space. Getting the camera. I'll leave the casting to Terry.

AMANDA FORSYTHE One of our current projects is to make DVD collections of works from the early years of Vidéo Populaire. I get a kick out of reading VidPop documents from the seventies. Terry will always say 'it was a different time and you had to be there.' I wish we could do that. Be there to get a handle on it. The artists are called '*membres-travailleurs*,' member workers.

Some of the videos are long by today's standards. Lots of long takes. I'm working on this with the Exhibitions coordinator, Éric Bellechasse, Terry and Nancy Amiot. We're trying to figure out which videos, which order and what kind of extras we can offer for educational purposes.

Terry and Lydia are available and ready to tape segments about different subjects. It's too bad that Maurice Aubert won't consent to being interviewed. I don't get that. It's a huge deal. I know that Maurice sees Lydia and Terry. I take it he has always been that way. I pitched this idea to Terry that maybe we could use photographs of Maurice and do a short documentary on him. Terry tells me there are no photographs except for one, unless Maurice himself has some.

I sent a registered letter to Carl-Yves, so I know he got it.

SERGE DUVAL I made five vidoes at Vidéo Populaire, all of them co-productions. My work in the nineties was on different subjects like the environment. I did one work on HIV/AIDS. I was so inspired by Robert and some of the other projects. I was obsessive. I taped different news broadcasts in French and English every day for about a year. Everytime AIDS was mentioned in any context, I would keep that footage. I also extended it to compile headlines from newspapers. I had a lot of material that I edited together to make a fifteen minute video. It's a barrage of sound bytes. Some people said some seriously dumb and ignorant things about HIV.

LYDIA CARTWRIGHT There was always that divide between film and video. The argument went, maybe still goes: film was so beautiful, had a history, was worthy of study. And video comes along in the sixties, looking cut-rate, fuzzy, a kind of not-TV. I actually love the quality of early video. Now of course video is studied, too. The ultimate revenge is that digital images mean that film and video are converging. People make work on video technology and say 'my film.' I won't surprise you by saying that video was for us non-bourgeois. The notion of video being tied to television and television technology has made the whole video-as-poor-cousin to TV and film epitaph a hard one to dismiss. When America's Funniest Home Videos started airing, I actually thought 'that's it, we lost' for a moment.

For us in the beginning video technology meant freedom. The means of production was in our hands. I can't emphasize that enough, when you shot something and could look at it right away, replay it, wow. No delay, like with film.

I don't know how many panels I've been on over three decades that asked the question, 'What is the future of video?' One thing for sure, video hasn't died. There was one panel Terry and I were invited on in the nineties. I remember thinking we were being trotted out as these poor old passé Marxists. Terry had more of an inkling of what we were getting into. He didn't talk at all. He just used his allotted time on the panel to show excerpts of videos from the VidPop collection. It was perfect. No one expected to see these lovely experimental pieces from the fucking *autocritique* brigade. I think we may have had a few converts that night.

I was the only woman at VidPop for a long while and this was from the beginning. Others joined later. Board members. Staff. The guys were, frankly, good guys. They might not have come to feminism on their own, but they got a bit of it, and sometimes more than got it. Terry and Carl-Yves had studied their oppression, knew their way around revolutions. Maurice was always just such an odd guy. I would say he got it, too, but it was just so hard to know what he thought and how he felt. He never said much. Once, I remember, he just came over and gave me a quick hug. I took that hug to mean a lot of things then, that he appreciated me, that he liked my work, that he somehow supported me. Don't really know. I felt like I knew guys like Moe. I have three brothers. My father was still alive back then, of course. There were a bunch of silent guys in my family. It was like my mother and I just kept the conversation going between us. My brothers and father weren't sullen, just very, very quiet. I'm comfortable around that. If someone doesn't talk, I don't feel weird.

Moe didn't ignore you. He listened. Sometimes he even said a few words. When he did, boy did I take note. I often got the feeling he was kind of willing us to understand his thoughts, so he wouldn't have to talk at all.

Carl-Yves was the only one who left, slamming the door, but there is a nuance to that. We got together in 1974, founded VidPop. The first three years were tough, but I think we all felt good. I know I did. We all had our things and we each brought our interests to the group and we decided together what we would work on. We were together practically all the time. I was in touch with some women who wanted to work on a video about rape. Carl-Yves had a friend who worked in a textile plant and he wanted to make a tape on workers' rights and I think there was the hint of a strike coming up and he was very excited. The strike happened, too, and Carl made his tape called *Le travail*. Brilliant.

Moe always did his own thing in his own way. I mean that he was a socially conscious guy and supported our interests and causes, but his work was experimental, abstract even, early on. He worked with feedback and even invented a few machines that would attack the video signal. Those Moechines, I tried them out, he showed me what to do but I wasn't into it or I wasn't good with them. I guess you could say the rest of us were more purist, representational, trying to show things as they were. In a way, Terry was right in the middle, making work about social issues, but also incorporating some art video things. And that was the beginning of the end right there. Carl was adamant that video was a tool for social change. For him, video had to be used for that or not at all. At first, he didn't mind Moe's videos, saw them as all part of what we were trying to do.

But the more Carl got involved in looking at unions and striking workers and the working poor, he had less and less patience for videos that didn't say anything. That's what he would say about Moe's videos towards the end, these don't say anything. They said something, they said a lot, but Carl wouldn't see it.

They were close, those two, Carl and Moe. They would do things for each other. Maurice was better on camera than Carl and they would head off to a factory or a meeting together. Moe would get all the shots Carl wanted in the way he wanted them. And Carl would say 'Y savait c'que je voyais.' Again, they barely talked. But they used to sit and Carl would roll a cigarette, hand it to Moe. Moe would open a beer and pass it to Carl, no talking. When they did talk, it sometimes became an argument. One sided, mostly. Carl would just hammer at Moe about being true to the cause and other stuff, that Moe's videos were anti-revolutionary, that he should work on things that contributed to social change. Mind you, almost right up until Carl left, Moe did camera for him and often edited his work. As way out as his own work could be, Moe could follow the fall line of an interview and pull out the key bits. Carl was a so-so editor of his own stuff and he knew it. He always wanted to leave everything in. Sometimes that's great, but not all the time.

I have begun to think about something regarding the relationship between Carl and Moe. Carl-Yves Dubé was from Québec City, Limoulou. His family was Francophone, and he spoke only French though he understood English and *could* speak it. Maurice Aubert was from Montréal, Outremont, a very nice neighbourhood, his father was Francophone, but originally from France, and his mother was Anglophone. Moe spoke English and French perfectly well. Carl came to see Moe as someone to fight against, you know, and not just because of his experimental videos. Not fight against, no, someone to pick at. Maurice was someone who could navigate in both worlds, French and English, and who came from privilege. He was with us politically, the separation of Québec from Canada, but he didn't mind switching to English. In fact, he said it wasn't switching for him, both languages were in his head.

Moe wasn't like that, wasn't that guy who expected things because he had grown up more wealthy than us, but Carl started to fixate on things like that. I think Carl began to categorize us, or maybe even see us as symbols of social ills. Terry was an Anglo who became a nationalist but who could never overcome his essential Angloness and his kind of political timidity. I was also an Anglo, also a nationalist, and a feminist, and Carl, while he supported women's rights, he thought those should come after all the other rights had been won. And Moe was a kind of semi-traitor, neither English nor French, and from a swanky neighbourhood, a Maurice who sometimes called himself 'Moe.' Carl only ever called him Maurice and sometimes ignored us if we asked 'Have you seen Moe?' That's just conjecture on my part, but it would have been a very Carl thing to do. So Carl sets himself up as the true defender of this Québécois video collective. For a while, I felt bad because I thought with him gone it would be easier to get more women involved. Then I felt bad for feeling bad, why did I need to defend my suggestions to Carl?

And Carl-Yves. It's like he just vanished there for a while. For several years, Terry and I even actively looked for him. We once went to this tavern he used to hang out in and found some guy he used to bring to VidPop events, some drinking buddy of his called Steve. If he knew how to get in touch with Carl, he never told us. We even considered hiring a private detective. Years later I remember thinking that we had figured Maurice was fragile but I was kind of worried about Carl, too.

I used to wonder where his convictions brought him or didn't. I could see him living in the country. When it was possible to Google, we tried that. I remember I dropped in on Terry at VidPop and we fell into conversation. We ended up Googling Carl-Yves Dubé. We had a good laugh because there was one guy who was a priest in Gaspé. I actually thought it could be him, that he had become a priest, one of those socially conscious ones, but there was a photo. So not him. Carl is a super popular name in Québec and so is Yves, but putting them together is rare.

CARL-YVES DUBÉ Maurice was a great cameraman and editor. I wasn't always the best judge of my own work. I needed help because I always wanted to keep everything I shot. Some directors get away with that, leaving most everything in. I wanted to, but it didn't work that way for me. Maurice would show me my version first, the one I insisted on, leaving almost everything in. Then he would show me the version he saw. Perfect. I'm much more ruthless with other people's work.

I probably was such a windbag then. I was not the only one. The endless monologues about this or that by Terrence or Lydia were *pénibles*. And believe me, we were three windbags in a large sea of windbags. Being with Maurice was calming.

Some artist even did a cartoon, a caricature of us four at Vidéo Populaire. I hope Terrence still displays it there. The cartoon has us all with those speech bubbles and we are all going on about different subjects and not listening to each other. No speech bubble for Maurice: blank.

I left for a lot of reasons. It was lots of things. I think the others will remember it as being mainly about him (Maurice) always getting his way and being in the way. But he was my comrade. I agonized over my decision. I went back and forth because we were kind of a team within a team. I came very close to changing my name. I always like that phrase 'hiding in plain sight' and that's what I tried to do.

I recognize what I was then. Frankly, I was *exécrable*. And disillusioned, which is a bad combination. I was so excited by the promise. It isn't our fault or Vidéo Populaire's 'fault' that things didn't come to be what we had hoped for. That was it for me, though. I tried but I had to give up because it was too hard. I couldn't accept the facts. It came down to being asked where 'Moe' was one too many times. We weren't the Three Stooges and we weren't Anglo.

DAVID SUMMERVILLE I didn't speak to Carl-Yves at all in the final weeks apart from saying 'salut.' I wasn't scared of him but he was so messed up he stopped me cold. I was really invested in them staying all together. The place was a new experience for me, a place that accepted my weirdness, and I didn't want it to change. I've always been a drama queen and poor Terrence and Maurice actually consoled me. Very sweet. I should have been consoling them. But that's what that place was for many of us, a place where you could go and hang with other freaks doing unusual things.

LOUIS CARON I realized I didn't have any interest in making videos myself. Carl-Yves was one of my buddies back then. He wanted me to get involved. I helped out where I could when one of them was working on something. I carried things, held microphones. I drifted away after a few years. I wasn't into it the way he wanted me to be. There was one thing, though, I was attracted to how committed they were. I hung around because of that feeling.

TERRENCE O'MEARA I made copies of Carl-Yves's videos to send to a curator recently.

It took some time, but there is an interest now in documentaries from the seventies. People said 'outdated' a decade ago. Now they are records of another time. Important. Very rigorous. Intellectual, his stuff. Sometimes intentionally funny even with all the Marxist analysis.

I mean what I said just now, that people were saying how old the videos seemed and then how prescient. How does that happen? I never seem to get the trends right.

ROSEMARY DRUMMOND Oh, we are all our own little archivists, right? Who cares about my sucky childhood but me? Who remembers the blue party dress I covered in mud fifty some years ago? I'll tell you who, me and my mother but she's gone now, so just me. That's it. That's my point. I carry all these VidPop stories in my head but unless I'm prompted, half of them stay in there!

NANCY AMIOT The idea somehow was that they were in the process of learning and trying to invent a new...maybe not a video language but perhaps a form. The video to see is the one they all collaborated on, *Vidéo-poème pour le Québec*. You can see that they are learning as they are going. Terry told me that Carl-Yves had seen *Four More Years* by TVTV and was heavily influenced by that kind of work. There was this spirit of anti-television, alternative television even. They believed that VidPop productions would be shown on TV. And some of them were.

Carl-Yves seems to be the one who was also most interested by what was going on in video elsewhere in Canada and even in the States. The case has been made that video history is very different from region to region. I would even say from centre to centre.

Carl wrote a really great text for *Le travail* and narrated it himself. It's not so obvious now but the fact that he narrated in *joual* was a pretty radical decision back then. He does a good job. It's the opposite of what people expected authoritative voices in documentaries to sound like.

ISABELLE MERCIER-LALONDE I worked in a factory back then. We made hosiery. My father was a union man. He brought me up to believe in worker's rights. I met Carl-Yves because he came to see us at the factory. He knew someone else who was working there. There were a few guys named Michel. I think he knew one of them. He would show up, sometimes alone, sometimes with Maurice and he would hang out with us at lunch. He brought the video camera one time. He put it on the table. He opened the box. He started talking about how it worked. Maurice picked it up and demonstrated. They put it back in the box. Carl kept showing up over a few months, regularly. He eventually talked about video and how he thought you could only make a documentary from within somehow, not from outside, that's what he always said, not from outside. He asked who was interested in forming a working group to document what was going on at the factory. We were gearing up for something. Don't think that this was all invisible, under the radar: the management was watching us and for sure they did notice these guys who would show up.

CARL-YVES DUBÉ I was reading a lot of things about making documentaries. I was a big fan of *Société nouvelle*, *Challenge for Change*, the ideas more than the results sometimes, but some of those films are just amazing. *VTR St-Jacques*! Beautiful.

I went to the Cinémathèque to see work by Joris Ivens, Eisenstein of course, my hero, and Pudovkin. Vertov. Chris Marker. I needed to be schooled. Godard. His *La Chinoise* is one of my favourite films. At the time, I just loved it and wanted to be part of that, to make something that effective.

I think I really shocked Lydia by liking the work of Nam June Paik. It was so different from my constant political message. But there is something utopic about his videos. There is an expansiveness and joy that just gets to me. I'm assuming you have seen *Global Groove*. Maurice and I agreed on him, too. I'm surprising myself now, too, by looking at videos I hated from the seventies. I show lots of older work to my classes now. Including Maurice's.

I just thought there we were in a time where everything was changing in our society — language, class, politics, religion — so that meant our job had to be to make videos that reflected those changes. That showed the chaos and all. From the inside. We used to watch those old voice-of-god narration documentaries and laugh. Took notes and made promises to each other to make a very different kind of documentary.

MAURICE AUBERT I'm always obsessed by an artist or artwork or art movement. Picabia, of course. Maya Deren. Shirley Clarke. Joyce Wieland. Sidney Peterson. General Idea. Many, many, many more. Oh, I shouldn't even list names because it just makes me feel bad for leaving people out. I watched all of the videos that Carl told me to and all the ones I wanted to.

ANTONIO DUTTO Carl was always giving me names of videos that I should watch. Lydia would come up to me after Carl had handed me a list and cross off titles and scold Carl because he was always giving people homework, like, watch this don't watch that.

In 1976 those four drove down to Pittsburgh to help us tape some of the first segments my brother Joe and I shot. I didn't ask them but Carl arranged it and they all came. It meant so much. It took a while for me to realize that we weren't working on one twenty-minute video. It was a series and it was Joe who decided. We made one a year, from 1976 until 1992, and Joe decided when it was over, too. My brother was not always good company. But sometimes he was and I got to experience that because we kept at it. Joe said about Maurice 'that guy looks shell-shocked.' And Joe would have known.

ISABELLE MERCIER-LALONDE Carl would tell me about videos. It wasn't my thing. Watching documentaries. I would have had to go there, to Vidéo Populaire, to see them. I didn't have too much free time between work, the union and my kid.

The way he explained it to us, he saw what we were doing as a document of a typical work cycle, condensed. Him and Maurice could shoot some of it from outside, across the street, but a lot of it would be actually shot by one of us in the working group. The camera and microphone were not invisible. We made a schedule so that someone would be shooting before or after one of the foremen had done their rounds. There were some close calls. Not everyone liked what we were doing. I told Carl and Maurice that we couldn't do this for months or even weeks. It had to be quick. We would be caught. I used the camera myself to get the women coming into the changing room in the morning. There was a locker room for women and one for men. Just their feet, just their hands, no faces. It was a relief when we had the footage from inside the factory. Then we concentrated on the union meetings we were having before and after the lockout.

MAURICE AUBERT   I was never good at strategy. I didn't know you needed a strategy. Terry and Lydia became great at it, a team that made VidPop part of all these initiatives and committees. I would figure things out long after the fact so I wasn't much use. Terry would always say to me we had different strengths. Ahead of the curve, that's the expression. I'm always in the curve or behind it. The other one is the glass half full or half empty. I can't even find my glass.

There was talk back then about the possibility that some videos we made would get shown on TV. I mean, we didn't watch TV, didn't like it, but we were convinced we could change it. Cable TV meant something way different back then. Carl-Yves and Lydia were working on an idea for a cable show with some other artists from Montréal. There would be a host and interviews with artists and some videos would be presented. There were discussions they had...they didn't want to reproduce standard TV. As if showing stuff like we were making would suddenly identify us as these broadcast sell-outs. That still makes me laugh. If you saw something by Carl or Lydia or me or Terry you would definitely not mistake it for regular programming.

LYDIA CARTWRIGHT   Carl wasn't at all sure it was a good idea to go that route, to appear on the medium that we were so against. We deliberated over that television project. We didn't want to reproduce TV. There was a whole movement of artists now able to use TV against itself by taping images and re-cutting them. In the end, we spent a long time developing our program ideas with other artists and groups, but our project was probably too unwieldy for TV. I can't say I was that sorry it didn't work.

CARL-YVES DUBÉ   That project was doomed from the start. We became involved but we did it more as an exercise. Would they really have let us have an hour to do exactly as we wished with no censorship? It seemed for a while there that TV opened up a bit. Then the doors slammed shut again. Soap operas. Bad comedies. Cop shows. It was good for video, though, fighting for its place. Lots of smart people had good ideas about showing videos in non-traditional spaces. I've seen videos in parks, projected on ice blocks, in abandoned buildings.

LOUIS CARON I had a television. Not everybody did back then. Carl-Yves used to ask me if I could actually justify watching it when it was all state propaganda. We were pals, high school buddies, you know, pot and skipping class. He got very serious about video. He would tell me that if his intent wasn't clear he would make something inferior and that was unacceptable.

NANCY AMIOT If they had stayed stuck in one decade, we wouldn't be talking about them quite so much now. They adapted. New artists came in later and brought new ideas. VidPop tried to develop a structure that corresponded to how they felt about art and politics. They were hip in the early years. And then they were kind of ridiculed. But people were being so reductive with VidPop. They were always more than Marxist-Leninist leanings and documentaries.

Right now these two young women are working on a video there because they won the Vidéo Populaire prize at their year-end screening. They have access to equipment for a month. The idea of access has been part of their mandate since the beginning.

AMANDA FORSYTHE After we have made DVD compilations of the founding members, I would like to move on to important artists involved with Vidéo Populaire. For the Sepúlvedas, I think it would be key to include some of their early Super 8 films. They went on to make a variety of documentaries, together and separately. Lorenzo is working on a feature fiction project.

Pierre Nadeau has five videos of his own but his name comes up in the credits for Carl-Yves, Maurice, Antonio Dutto, Rosemary.

BEVERLY CAMPBELL The collection was a mess. Back then, the late nineties, we were still dealing with $^{3}/_{4}$" tapes even though there were other formats, too. They took up a lot of room. We had shelving built to accommodate...I think we were distributing about 400-500 works by then. It was a smaller collection than other video and film centres.

Some of the themes were outdated, like *Class Struggles*. I understand that was important in the seventies but you have to remember I was trying to standardize the themes and put some order in the collection. It wasn't that I wanted to throw old labels out but I wanted to know how best to represent the collection. One of the main focuses was to review the classification system VidPop had, which had been developed to reflect the interests and politics of the seventies. Terry was cool with the changes. He supported the shift because he wanted VidPop to be current. I wasn't a specialist or anything like that so I suggested we get someone to help us who was studying Library Technology at McGill.

TERRENCE O'MEARA Sometimes I feel like I'm channeling Carl-Yves circa 1974. Or that I want to channel him. I get that a collection should be properly catalogued. Sometimes I think, though, that we might be erasing something unique. It's not about dwelling in the past. So what if we have subjects in our index that no one else has? We also have a history that no one else has. To really know video history in Québec and Canada, I feel you would have to get to know the history of each centre.

LYDIA CARTWRIGHT Terry sells himself short. I know this is not what he wants to hear, but he is solid. Without him, there would be no retrospective screenings of VidPop or of Maurice's or anyone's work. He keeps it all together. He teaches courses now at two of the universities. He could do that full time, but he's never fully wanted to leave the centre. I wish someone would look at his tapes and write about them. It's always been Maurice first, then Carl-Yves, then me and somehow Terry's own videos are rarely considered. But they should be.

I knew when it was time to leave. I knew it but ignored the feeling. I had stuck with something for the first time. Then I started feeling that I had done what there was to do and I should do other things. I was there off and on for about fifteen years. Not an easy decision. And I think it took me almost a year to make it stick. When I first left, I stayed away for a long time.

After starting my M.A., I decided to attend a few VidPop events, screenings, maybe, or a fundraiser. Anyhow, it was okay. Weird, but okay, and seeing Terry and some of the others was great. I had to take a step back.

Now, sometimes when Terry wants advice he gets in touch with me. I feel somewhat removed from VidPop but really protective of it, too. Typical. And now that time has passed I sometimes volunteer. Or I'll take on a project.

For a few years at least, Terry and I kept in touch with Maurice. It was always one of us initiating contact, never Maurice. I kind of saw him regularly until the nineties. Now, we see each other about once a year. The best gift to bring Maurice is video art.

TERRENCE O'MEARA I thought it would be nice if we could end VidPop like *Longtime Companion* — every dead friend ends up on the beach and everyone embraces. Of course I also find that ending manipulative and odd even though I cried the first time I saw it. But so great somehow for VidPop. I spent a long time searching for Carl-Yves. I wanted to know what happened to him. I started to think he might actually be hiding. Not the same thing at all, but could he be like Moe, living just blocks from VidPop?

Carl will probably have other stories and most definitely a different take on the ones I'm telling. Did he soften up? Are his political views the same? Or is he wearing a suit somewhere making some serious money? I think anything is possible. I guess I would really like a reunion.

I single-handedly ended the custom of having a record

player at VidPop. It was being used for people to bicker and pick at each other through songs. I couldn't stand it anymore, just took the thing home with me. I can still see Carl standing in the spot where the record player used to be, holding an album by Octobre, ready to play it at us.

Carl-Yves kicked a representative from an arts funder out of our office once. The guy had come to announce some changes to a grant. This was way back. Maybe 1980. He came into our office and I guess he was one of those people who liked his video to be art. He wasn't getting the social issue stuff. Was it his place to tell us that? I don't remember enough about the event to know if he was relaying jury comments or if this was just his opinion. Carl listened to this guy for a while then he laced into him. Told him what he thought about his nebulous division between art and documentary. Told him VidPop was big enough for Maurice and his way of making work and other practices. I remember thinking two things. The first was to make Carl shut up because this guy represented a place that gave us money. If I'm not mistaken, it was three thousand dollars. And I thought Carl had it absolutely right even though the yelling and swearing was a bit much. Carl sometimes really did have a cloud hovering over his head. It obscured everything else. But he was right to let that guy have it. Carl could always energize me.

MAURICE AUBERT I found an old Barco projector in an alley. Someone just put it out with the garbage. They don't make them anymore. I thought I could get it to work. It's an old kind with three different coloured lamps like headlights. I remember how we used to really have to work to get a Barco to focus.

It works now. And I didn't have to do much. The lights are blinding if you look at them too long. I set the Barco up facing a wall.

I sit and watch the beams of light shooting out. This projector used to be the best thing, but there are better machines out there now. You wouldn't find those outside in an alley. The hum it makes reminds me of old furnaces and basements.

Sometimes if I can't sleep, I get out of bed and turn the Barco on. It can never be pitch black here, not unless there is a power blackout. There is a streetlight just outside my front window.

I sit on the floor and look at the beams against the wall. There is a shape that is projected...a kind of oval, but with wavy lines. I checked to see if one of the big eyes, the blue, red or green, has a defect shaped like an oval. None of them does. I'm a bit freaked out. Maybe there is something in the Barco. That shape is strange.

You know those old, old cameras, the first ones to come out, they were magic, because if you were lucky enough to be around then they had a promise that you could make something immediately. You can't go back to that. The new ones aren't about promises.

TERRENCE O'MEARA When Moe left it took me a while to figure out he had really gone. He just drifted away. We kept things going. To be frank, Moe was not the most productive member. I mean, he contributed so much, but the guy would not answer a phone or type a grant. He did his own work. And he took care of our equipment. I answered the phone. I typed the grants. Then it was his presence. The machines felt different, like they weren't getting their workout or something. Some of that Moe old black magic stuff around machines. We may have had a meeting where we told him he had to do more. Just because he was a founding member didn't mean everything was free for him. That was very hard to do. After he left, the edit suite was empty. Word got out, I guess, that he wasn't in there all the time anymore and artists started coming in to do their work.

Sometimes I think Carl-Yves and I could have a conversation like the one between Harrison Ford and Rutger Hauer in *Blade Runner*. I guess I would be the one dangling from the building and Carl would get the good line.

In other projects besides VidPop, I always was raring to

go and get some work done, some writing or a video series I was trying to make happen. I think I let VP just fill up my time. It was easy. There is always tons to do. Always some strategy to devise. Defend the existence of your centre. Why are you still relevant? Grants. Screenings. Meetings. Workshops. Catalogues. And it seems as if this is it for me. Even without the other three.

I teach classes at Concordia and UQAM and work at VidPop. It's turned out to be a good balance for me. Slowly, I'm prepping my leaving and how to set up the transition. There will be a lot of details but at one point I will just have to say 'this is it.' The current board knows. When we hire a new coordinator, I will accompany her or him for a month or so. It's not like it used to be. It's not just me overseeing everything.

I love movies. Feature films. All kinds. I watch as many as I can. I thought I wanted to make them, movies. I realized that each time I made a video, the natural end was seventeen minutes. After that, it was all too much and it wasn't any good. I tried to pad my videos, go to twenty minutes, but everyone would say 'oh, just cut that out, it doesn't work.' Seventeen minutes.

LYDIA CARTWRIGHT I regret saying to Terry that he was an 'extra man.' He brings it up sometimes. But I meant it as a compliment. Terry is so courtly. It's like he comes from another time. I think he tends to see it as a put-down. Believe me, when you were surrounded by guys who were jumping around to be the centre of attention, someone like Terry was great.

I just started thinking of him as the decent guy in some of those old films, the ones that get thrown over for some more dangerous man. Personally, I think it is incredible that he is still at VidPop. I don't see it as weird or a failing. Out of all of us, he had the strength to keep going.

PIERRE NADEAU I took a break. I knew it would cost me so much but I had to go. I went to Mexico for a few years in 1981. I just picked up and left. I told my mother and no one else. I was spending too much time at Vidéo Populaire and not enough at UQAM. Carl was not doing well. He was working on a documentary called *La grève* and I was doing some camera for him. Maurice was the main cameraman. Carl would go back and forth on whether Maurice was committed enough to the cause. Going to VidPop was not the charge it used to be. I know now he was in the middle of fighting with himself about leaving or staying. I couldn't watch it anymore, frankly. I thought he was going to take everyone down with him. But he didn't. I know his was a bad departure but somehow he had the grace not to set fire to the whole thing. I went away and mourned the end of the video/social revolution. I thought I was probably mourning the end of VidPop but I was wrong about that. When I came back in 1983, I was amazed to hear about them, that they were still around. I had an image in my head that the building they had been in would be gone, demolished, exploded. It was weird but it was what I saw. I went to prove myself wrong. No Carl of course, no Carl ever again at VidPop, but the place was still standing and I have to say I was surprised to find myself feeling quite overjoyed.

LUISA SEPÚLVEDA Pierre Nadeau sought me out. I was a bit less involved, basically attending events by then and mostly going to school. Lorenzo was shattered by the fact that Carl-Yves left and cut off all ties for a while. They were close. He saw Carl as a mentor. There was no need to choose, I thought. You could love Carl-Yves and still support VidPop. Lorenzo eventually returned. This was a few years before Maurice left, too.

ISABELLE MERCIER-LALONDE I didn't want my name on the video. No one from work did. We told Carl-Yves just put your name and the *Comité des travailleurs de l'usine Brompton*. He was really upset. He wanted it to be all of us together credited. I told him we were autonomous, we had met and voted. It wasn't about proper credit, it was about showing what our factory work was like.

Carl organized preview screenings of the video before it was completed. A bunch of us would go to Vidéo Populaire and watch it then comment. Maybe that happened four or five times. We made suggestions and next time there they were, the changes, in the version he showed us.

Carl-Yves wanted me to get involved there, at Vidéo Populaire. I never did because I had no time. That's my only contribution to a video production. No, later Carl asked me to be a consultant for another of his videos.

BEVERLY CAMPBELL When I started work, there were boxes that hadn't been opened in years. I did open them and there were some one-inch open reel tapes and other dead formats. Unlabelled, most of them. I asked Terry if he thought they might have been migrated and he didn't remember. I was smelling the vinegar smell of a disintegrating tape so I told him we had to do something. He is bizarre around the old stuff. I wasn't sure he was making considered decisions and I told him that. I sent a tape to be migrated without even consulting him. 'Rosemary' was written on the label. Turns out it was footage that Rosemary took for an unfinished video. It's a performance she did called 'I apologize,' so a pretty important discovery! Just lying around.

We had ³/₄" tapes, VHS, Betacam SP, a really solid format that seemed to last, and when I left we were just thinking about DVDs. Terry already hated DVDs. He thought the format was useless. He preferred VHS and I could see his point. I made the suggestion that we could display some of the old cameras in a glass cabinet at the entrance.

ROSEMARY DRUMMOND Terrence is perfect except when he's not. He runs that place really well, always has. Everybody fucks up. I guess it was my responsibility to make sure things I did back then made it to the 21st century. Who knew I would even care? Who knew that there would be so many format changes? I did this performance in which I apologized for a bunch of things, being too smart, being overweight, the Vietnam war, the dictatorship in Chile and so on. Thanks to Bev, I saw it again. Piece of shit.

TERRENCE O'MEARA I used to worry a lot about Maurice. I don't know. He never said much, but there were times when his whole appearance changed. His face would sink in on itself.

He's had a hard time of it. Believe me, when you talked about things like that in the seventies and eighties, people hadn't taken their sensitivity training yet. I include myself in that comment. We had a tendency to think it was a character flaw. 'Pull yourself up by your bootstraps.' Moe was showing signs of distress. Did I think that when he left? No, I was just so upset that it was over, our amazing group that we had created. It was Lydia who brought it up. We would try to visit Maurice regularly. She talked about agoraphobia. I admit that I thought that only happened to women. Believe me, she set me right. We went to see him together not that long ago. Lydia brought along work by some of her students. We watched those together. He loves looking at work by new artists. Maurice even made us something to eat from his current list of foods. Avocado something.

When I really got depressed was after Lydia left. I understood then. It just happened to me the once, really badly, but you don't get it unless you're in it.

GUILLAUME R. BOIVIN I liked it there back then in the early eighties. You could drop in for a beer and hang out. Terrence could be unbearable. So pious. Maurice was a fucking loon. He liked a brand of soda, Pop Shoppe, and one flavour, the green one, had to be lime something. I can still see the colour. He would have a case of the stuff and drink it like water. People smoked everywhere back then. Once I edited a video at VidPop. I was there for weeks. I had to kick Maurice out of the edit suite constantly. I mean, you would take the trouble to book time and the fucker would just keep going in as if he was the only one. They were so boring when it came to politics, so serious. Endless meetings. Mao this. Marx that. I was never a member. I just accessed the services and equipment. It's still around though, that's something, when so many other places are gone.

That fucker Carl-Yves. He disappeared with some of my footage. I still have an unfinished video because of him. If you ever wanted Carl-Yves to turn into a monster before your eyes, you just had to whisper something about his politics or Laurent, that poet.

I edit peoples' work now, mostly documentaries.

Do you know what it was like to edit back then? You made a mistake, you started over. You realized your tenth shot was actually your third shot and it was back to square one. No cut and paste, there, problem solved. Analogue, *hostie*. Took the time it took. It took several people to cue tape on various machines so that another person could press record on another machine. And you didn't always get it perfectly right.

CARL-YVES DUBÉ I did some camera work for a guy who called himself RGB. No comment. He had given me three... I don't remember which format of cassettes. I was going to Trois-Rivières for a *manif* and he couldn't go. I shot two cassettes worth of footage for him. And one for me. I got what he asked me for. As far as I'm concerned, I owed him one blank tape. I bought one and gave it to him. He always contended that all the tapes were his, because I was working for him that day. He claims I did better work for myself. And on and on about his unfinished work that I ruined!

Nadeau was mixed up in that RGB mess somehow. I never forgave Pierre for abandoning the cause, dropping my project *La grève* and going to Mexico. He never even told me. Just disappeared. There were all kinds of rumours. I even went to his apartment to make sure he wasn't sick or worse. Oh no, I thought, not another death. We were working on something, it seems to me. We were in the middle of something. I was so furious that I felt like I was botching *La grève*. I couldn't concentrate. Maurice saved whole sections of that video. He could see. I couldn't, I was so *enragé*. Finally we hear Nadeau is in Mexico.

Mostly I started to hate RGB because he wasn't respectful to Maurice. Lydia had good insight, as usual. She used to say something about how we were all cool, all misfits, all counterculture, but a few types would slip into Vidéo Populaire and scorn...or pity Maurice. They didn't last long. They didn't understand that we were a collective in more ways than one. I would take Dr. Tim over people like RGB any day. Tim probably didn't always get us, but he sure accepted us.

I hadn't realized I was having arguments with people in my head. Lydia caught me muttering to myself one too many times. I hated appearing that way to her. I thought at first I was beginning to hate her but it wasn't that at all. I think some of my venom was just leaking out of me.

TERRENCE O'MEARA I haven't thought about RGB in years. He came close to hitting me once because he was going on about Carl-Yves stealing something from him, some idea... or some images...

If I remember correctly, after he told me that Carl had 'stolen' from him, I think I started talking about famous movie directors who had worked around missing or damaged footage. RGB got this look in his eyes and just took a swing at me. Shut up, Terry. Lydia would sometimes write that on a piece of paper at meetings and pass it to me. With a smiley face. It wasn't mean. It was to let me know I was going on too long.

Those two, Carl and RGB. I've never understood how you can be such good friends and then sworn enemies. Same with Carl and Pierre Nadeau. Carl and me. Carl, Maurice. Carl, Lydia. I still think that Carl has sworn enemies. And then he has us.

LOUIS CARON This woman, Nancy, found me and got in touch with me because she had seen my name in the credits of quite a few of those videos. I didn't always have a role but I guess the directors thanked me. I told her this one thing. We handwrote the credits because there was no way to generate text in the early years. So the cardboard with my name on it, it's me who wrote it out. We each wrote our names and held them up to the camera. That's why she talked to me. I wrote out my name and Maurice shot it.

ELSA SMITH I want them to do a big 40th anniversary party. I want to see everyone. I'm also hoping that some of the characters I never met will show up. My partner thinks I'm exaggerating about some of the people I knew. Wait until she sees them.

ROBERT T. ROBERTS I kind of went around the world with *Dream One* because it was selected at all these queer festivals and some experimental festivals. On a couple of occasions, people would ask me about VidPop. I guess this would have been more video people who knew a bit about the place or maybe had even visited it. The questions were so out of left field for me, about things that had happened before I set foot at VidPop. This French guy in Brussels asked me whether it was true that Maurice dropped acid to edit. Somebody else asked how much time the founding members had spent in jail for some murder.

CARL-YVES DUBÉ I didn't want Vidéo Populaire to be a magnet for lost people who didn't know what to do with their lives. They couldn't fit in or hold a straight job so come on over and join the outcasts. Terrence used to talk about a vocation and I agree. At least have some spark in you. Even Dr. Tim had that.

I tried to bury Vidéo Populaire. I needed to do it. It was like quitting everything — smoking, drinking, drugs, a relationship — all at once only more extreme. I just held tight until the feeling passed. I had this armchair and I squeezed the fabric right off the armrests.

It took forever. For years I'd had a place to go. I applied to university again. I forced myself to go to classes. I didn't care at first, but I went until I did care a bit. Honestly, I don't know how I got through. I broke up with everybody. I hadn't really been alone much in years. Vidéo Populaire was on St-Laurent and I tried never to go near there. I didn't make new friends until a few years later. The one main person I stayed in touch with was Isabelle. I saw her as safe because she was not so associated with Vidéo Populaire. I owe her a lot because she would get annoyed with me and tell me to snap out of it, I wasn't special. I tried to cut ties with Tim, but he wouldn't let me. He kept at me.

Nothing was going to change. We were going to go on holding up ideals. And things would just get worse. We were poor and would become poorer. But that didn't matter, it wasn't about money. And Vidéo Populaire would close because everyone got tired and all the arts funding dried up. I was wrong about a lot of things. The funding did not dry up though the current government is trying its best to curtail art making. When the student movement picked up recently and we had that whole great pot-banging spring, I almost wanted to pick up a camera again. My son was right into it and would show me images he shot on his phone. His phone. I showed him photos of me with the first cameras we had. Maurice, Lydia and me and we are all holding some piece of equipment because that's how it was in the seventies. And we thought that was portable. It was too short, too intense, the student protests.

Terrence was really adamant about having us recruit new members when we left. I was *baveux* and said 'like a replacement Carl-Yves, someone with actual politics? A nut job to replace Maurice? And for you, a *fonctionnaire*.' Terrence was so mad at me for those comments, he threw me out.

ROGER CROSS I didn't know much about independent video, I had gone to Concordia in film production and needed a job after getting my degree. Everything was print back then. We would put out a catalogue or supplement and mail it out. I would make cold phone calls. Hello, would you like to buy seminal videos from the seventies, we are having a special, this is true, two for the price of one! I started going to film festivals, markets, with information on our collection. It was like I was designing the job as I went along in a way. Terry was around part-time. We were always understaffed. It was me four days a week and barely paid, what else is new? There was Camille Soucy who coordinated equipment rental and production stuff. We had an active board. Some members would come and pitch in when we needed help, especially for writing grants.

When I started working there, we were using typewriters. Then we bought one Mac Classic. I can remember typing grants on the typewriter. When I would look in the old file folders to get ideas, I would find handwritten grants! Back then, we were going from Video 8 to Hi-8.

BEVERLY CAMPBELL I kind of fell in love with video while I was working at VidPop. I went to a screening that was held in an alley. Videos were projected on a white wall. Turns out it was VidPop. I thought the event was cool. To be frank, I didn't know much. I think Terry and the board hired me for my enthusiasm. I liked the job because I did a bit of everything. I would look at new work and recommend it to the acquisitions committee. I would sometimes travel around a bit with video programs. And then do regular grunt stuff like in real offices. I would have stayed longer but there were temporary money problems. It was no one's fault or anything, it was just a bad year for grants and no one was getting paid regularly. Terry was mortified, poor guy.

TERRENCE O'MEARA I wish it was possible for you to track down everyone that participated in VidPop. There was a young woman who came around to VidPop in the eighties for a year or so. Jeanne. Very smart and committed. She died in a car accident. Was it 1984?

I can't call up her face at all. I would need to see a photograph. Books were dedicated to her. Videos and films, too. She had many friends and a lot of them were beginning their careers as film or videomakers or writers. She was a student. I do remember that I wished VidPop could have paid her, kept her on staff. She was one of those people who...well, she figured things out very quickly. I didn't know her very well at all but I find myself thinking of her quite often these days.

That's just one person. Michel. Laurent, of course. For the first four years or so, we were not keeping great records. Board members, yes, and staff was easy, it was mainly us four. But people who came through the centre to make videos or take workshops or help out, no.

DR. TIMOTHY PETERSON I send something to Carl twice a year. 'It has been six months since your last check-up.' Sometimes I write him a short note.

LOUIS CARON When I was still going to VidPop, I wasn't hanging out with Carl-Yves so much anymore. He didn't have time. He never stopped moving. I would talk to Terry mostly. Maurice would let me sit with him as he edited. I admired the way he would kind of disappear into his editing.

You don't want to feel like you aren't welcome. I think Carl-Yves said something about contributing if I was going to keep showing up. It hurt my feelings. I didn't know what I could do. I didn't have any ideas to make videos. It's like it never occured to me to volunteer or put my name forward for the board. I stopped going.

MYLÈNE BOISJOLI I never lost touch with Carl-Yves. We didn't see each other for several years. I continued to receive postcards from him. The political slogans stopped. I went to a screening at Vidéo Populaire sometime in the mid-eighties. I was hoping to see him, but no, he was long gone. Lydia and Terrence filled me in.

Many of the things that happened at VidPop, the socio-political side, had also happened in theatre. I belonged to an experimental theatre troupe but I also played roles to earn my living. I got a job on a television show, a popular children's show. I was afraid that I would get a postcard from Carl-Yves with a condemnation. I actually went to VidPop to tell him about my new job, that he might see me in something mainstream. On the show, I played the role of a child who, with her two friends, constantly puts thing over on the mayor of their town. I thought I could sell it to him because it was vaguely anti-capitalist. I got a card from him. He called me by the name of my TV character, Mimi, and drew a heart and a hammer and sickle.

MAURICE AUBERT Some days I have to concentrate. I mean a ketchup bottle isn't menacing, right? We had all read our Orwell. I probably was still there in 1984. I think it was more likely 1985-86 when I left for good.

The last time we looked at videos together, Carl and I watched *The Eternal Frame* by Ant Farm and T.R. Uthco and *60 Unit Bruise* by Paul Wong. Carl was wondering about the media and Brechtian techniques for one of his works and he always, always looked at lots of videos as part of his research. I loved watching tapes with him. He watched videos the way some guys watched sports. When Ant Farm re-enacted the assassination of Kennedy in the video, Carl said 'tabernak, hostie' over and over and over. He was standing up and sitting down. He told me Kennedy's death had always seemed so far and remote but now he could see the impact of it in a way.

CARL-YVES DUBÉ I teach cégep students production and I also do some consulting for scripts and editing. I pick up cameras almost every day but to demonstrate techniques and shots. I shoot lots of footage but I don't make videos anymore. I feel like I would make the same video over and over. Maybe I would just make *Le travail* until I die. Or remake *La Chinoise* very badly. I couldn't face that.

I'm thinking of Terrence right now because when I said 'remake' I thought of the American version of *À bout de souffle*. Pointless.

I don't know how Terrence has done it for so long. Good for him. At the same time, I can't help thinking what a way to just squander yourself. I don't know, I feel strange about someone who just stayed on. I couldn't have done it. But Terrence was not falling from such a high place as me. I thought video was going to usher in a new order. At the very beginning in 1974 and 1975 and 1976 if someone had asked me I would have said I'd still be there in 2000. So I guess maybe I could understand in a way.

It isn't anyone's fault but mine. I have seven brothers and sisters. My father died at 57. My mother followed a few years later. I think they were just ground down by poverty. If I'd stayed in Québec City and done the work that some of my brothers did...I couldn't. I'm not saying they made bad choices. I'm probably saying they felt like they didn't have a choice. One *usine* or the other. I was looking for my cause and it was Nationalism. Through Marxism. Through video. It kind of all came together. That answered my questions back then. It was for me the tool to share ideas. I felt that.

The fights I had with Terrence and Lydia...I didn't pick them all. Fighting with Maurice was useless. He just shut down. He would get in a few words and stop. You could see him retreating inside. They were all moving away from our original mandate. Video as a tool for social change. I firmly believed that. Still do, I guess.

I went to a VidPop screening once. I know I can be so rigid. I heard it from people for years until I finally started seeing it in myself. I thought it would be a good exercise to see some of the old videos. It was in Ste-Foy, a church basement, in the early nineties. I was in Québec City, probably visiting my family. I made sure to slip in after the lights were off, just in case one of them was there. I sat in the back row. I spotted Terrence right away, sitting next to the projector. I froze. Once I saw him, all I could think about was that he would turn around and see me. There were probably twenty-five to thirty people there. I slid down in my seat and was sort of hidden by two people in front of me.

It seemed that Maurice's work hadn't aged, the little fucker! So amazing. When one of mine came up I remember my heart was just racing. So horribly dated in some ways. But some of the analysis in the video had caught up to the present or something like that. I was surprised. Lydia's piece was quite good. I never liked that kind of confessional work but I appreciated it that night. So smart.

I could see Terrence sitting near the front, his outline against the screen. I got distracted and kept watching his outline to make sure he didn't get up and come towards me in the back. I left before the end. During Maurice's video, someone stood up and just kept standing. At least no one screamed.

NANCY AMIOT Some organizations closed down due to funding. And some due to staff departures or mandate changes. VidPop has been remarkably resilient, I think because it has adapted. Also, the fact that it is a production, distribution and exhibition centre. When it became possible to edit on your home computer, quite a few production centres hit hard times or disappeared. It seems like they got it right by focusing almost equally on three areas.

I go regularly to screenings organized by VidPop because I think they are interesting right now. VidPop is taking such a close look at historical video. I've been asked to work on some 40th anniversary programs that will be shown in 2014. My secret wish is to get the four founding members to the inaugural screening. Good luck to me, right? We'll see. You know, each of them has a distinct style. And each one made at least one seminal video. I have actually been considering using videos as bait.

ROSEMARY DRUMMOND When there was that exhibition a few years ago, the one at *La maison des arts*, the one on video in the seventies, I took Maurice. That was a production, getting him there, but so worth it. The trick is to prepare him and then prepare him some more. It takes a bit of patience to get him out of the house. Hey, he put up with a lot of my crap over the years. I drove over to his place. We collected his water bottle, his paper bag, his book and his camera. He always has a camera. We took his dog, Yma Sumac. And we went. It took us a while to get there. We would stop at certain places, that's better for him, and Maurice would tape some footage.

When we got to the Maison, I took Yma for a walk and Maurice went in. It was a really good exhibition. Nancy Amiot did a nice job. They had set out old cameras and machines and they were playing videos that had been created by those same things. There was a section on Vidéo Populaire. Maurice loved it. He asked to go back again. Same procedure. Terry and Lydia and I went to the opening and we met Pierre Nadeau and Luisa Sepúlveda there. Terry had tried and tried to get Maurice to join us but you can't do that to Moe, you can't bring him to a vernissage with lots of people. Hello, Terry, don't you understand anything about your friend? Anyhow, Maurice spent hours there even though he knows just about everything there is to know about all that old video equipment and those tapes.

ISABELLE MERCIER-LALONDE Carl-Yves and I get together to this day. When he left Vidéo Populaire and was so down, I told him that his revolution would not come on a silver platter. I remember he asked me why I kept saying 'his revolution' and I told him he was always being selfish and self-centred...what he had wished for didn't belong only to him. It was hard for all of us. I told him he should come and work in the factory. I thought it would give him the perspective he needed and undo some of the knots in his head.

MAURICE AUBERT I can still see the images from then. Once a year Terry sends me money from screenings of my old videos. I used to get a cheque and a handwritten note from him. For years it was 'we should get together soon.' Then it was 'hope you are well'. Maybe if he gets to the point where he just puts a cheque in an envelope with no note, maybe then it will be over this thing he has about VidPop and me. And we can start something new. I don't cash the cheques. Just keep them. We see each other. He brings me news. Sometimes he brings me copies of work I might like. Lydia comes by, too.

Some days I have to follow some rules and I can't go above Rachel or below Duluth or past St-Laurent. Or St-Denis. VidPop is just off that grid. If we had rented that space on Duluth back then maybe things would have been different.

I put the Barco out on the sidewalk. Then I went and got it again. Maybe it belongs at VidPop. Maybe someone could do a screening with it, old tapes on an old projector.

First snow. It's hard when it comes in October. It came down all evening and all night long. I watched out my window as it swirled in the streetlight. I watched for a long time and sometimes followed lines up then down, into eddies, landing. That's why it came then, the thought that might lead somewhere. Watching the snow swirl.

I dream of my grandparent's house over and over. It is exactly as it was. I see it as I saw it, every detail, the carpet, the table, the candies in a bowl, the smell, the bunk beds, the light from the window.

LUISA SEPÚLVEDA Maurice and I have been talking about emulation. We got on the subject because of an exhibition catalogue he ordered. In order to show an interactive work from the eighties, these conservators worked with the artists to kind of mimic their original technology. Because in the eighties, the computer they used was very slow compared to what we have now. The artists had also written their own computer program to bring up random images at intervals. Now you touch a screen, boom, you have what you want. That isn't what these artists wanted — they wanted time and a slower pace. They wanted it as close to the original as possible. The catalogue explained all this and had images of the installation. Maurice said that he could have rigged something up for them. He has this younger friend who likes the old technology and they get together to talk machines.

LYDIA CARTWRIGHT One thing I can say without question is that VidPop made me. I thought I invested myself too much back then — we practically lived there — but it doesn't seem that way now. I got to sharpen my arguments, learn how to make videos, learn lots of things. Probably without VidPop, I might not have gone back to school and become a teacher. When I used to look back, I thought I was kind of aimless in my youth but it turns out I wasn't really. I mean sometimes we had no idea what we were doing but we were doing it.

No one broke up VidPop. It became an entity. In a way it proved stronger than all of us.

LISA HARROW I liked what they did and stood for. Once I cleaned and painted the walls. Everybody smoked back then. All the time. Bad for the videos and machines. I never did smoke. Now it's the opposite almost no one smokes. I remember trying to convince Terry that it was bad for all the videos never mind the people. We didn't have a vault or anything like that to keep the tapes in.

I think I hung around for four years or so. I would answer the phone, take bookings, make copies, clean up. If you volunteered a certain number of hours, you could get credit to use equipment. I took advantage of it. I made three tapes that way.

Terry was always kind, a nice guy, even-tempered. Lydia was around, less, but still involved. I met the legend, Maurice. Odd guy. He wouldn't say much but he would sometimes give me one of his lime soft drinks. I never met Carl-Yves. But I kind of got a sense of him from watching his videos and listening to people talk about him.

There were lots of meetings held in that space. Not all

of them had to do with running VidPop. Political meetings. Production meetings. Also meetings about things like distributing these independent videos. Meetings about guaranteeing artist fees. People dropped in. VidPop attracted people that wanted to learn editing or watch videos in the collection. Lots of stuff going on there and I always thought it was pretty vibrant and a little disorganized.

CARL-YVES DUBÉ The language thing. I was not the only one who thought it was important to speak my mother tongue. That idea was everywhere then. I appreciated the fact that Terrence and Lydia had learned French and made it the language used at Vidéo Populaire.

Sometimes I had to be patient at first. They wouldn't find their words. Or I would say something and they wouldn't get it. Maurice was the only one of us who was perfectly bilingual at first. The little fucker would take advantage of us! I would say 'en tout cas' which could be translated as 'anyhow' and he would do a terrible translation and tell Terry it meant 'in two cases.' We started using that term around VidPop as our joke. I used to tell Lydia when she could say 'quincaillerie' without stumbling she would be one of us. She got there eventually. Another hard one was 'Longueuil.' I used to ask Terrence to spell it.

MAURICE AUBERT The end of my time at VidPop was like crashing over and over again. I thought I could rely on the Dadaists, how much I loved them and their work, to get me through. But I couldn't. That was a terrible moment because they were a comfort to me for so long. But I would read about them and the idea of absurdity and chaos I guess was too much for me at that time. I had to give them up for a while.

I forgot how to sleep. I could barely eat. I forgot how to swallow but I guess I did because you have to.

I was afraid. Of stones, their insides and outsides, the shape of them, the space they took up, the absence of movement. Birds. Their flight. The silver light on their wings.

Winter. All by itself, just the word. But not just the word after you have said it, everything that follows the word.

My breath turned liquid. It swam in me. I never had enough air but by then I had too much. It flew out of me. I would gulp it back in.

I was even afraid of my Grandparent's old radio, which I still have. It glowed. It had big dial knobs I used to like to twist when I was a kid. I couldn't look at it for a long time. It was squat. It took up too much room. It expanded through static. I couldn't latch on to anything. Everything was tone. Spoons, too. I rarely use them even now.

I went on medication for quite a while. Until I had a dream. I think it was a dream. It was mostly a voice, speaking to me in a ripoff of T.S. Eliot.

> Shall I, shall I take my pill
> it's lovely blue unbidden
> I shall, I shall
> with a spot of milk
> and keep the swallow hidden

After that, I didn't want to take the pills anymore.

I've had times like that since, but never as bad. I give myself tasks, keep order, cook, ride my exercise bicycle, work on my tapes. My sister Danielle helps me very much. Marie, too. Rosemary always offers to drive me places. Lydia is a good person. Knowing Terry was close by was good. I got hooked on a TV show for the first time in my life. I felt so guilty watching *MacGyver* trying not to think of what Carl would say to me if he knew. Terry kept telling me it was okay, whatever made me feel okay was okay, even if it was bad TV. Much later when I was much better I got hooked on *The Teletubbies*. Talk about Dada.

DANIELLE AUBERT I went to see Maurice for our visit and he was in such terrible shape. I couldn't get anything out of him. The only thing in his life was the centre. The only thing. So I marched over to VidPop because I had to know. I still don't know exactly. Terrence says it was because the machines and configuration of the office was changing. And

Carl had left a few years before. Maurice says he felt a little like he was being pushed. At first he said 'pushed out' then later he just said 'pushed' and I told him I thought there was quite a difference. Terrence has always been good to my brother. He keeps in touch and visits him. He defends him. Lydia, as well. Maurice misses Carl-Yves, it's as simple as that. I don't suppose either of them could come up with a good reason why they don't talk to or see each other.

TERRENCE O'MEARA I used to think about it non-stop. Did we all stay together for the time that we did because of alchemy? I don't want to reduce everyone to one note here but if you think about Maurice then, he was the one who couldn't stop doing his work. It is absolutely true that people liked his work from the start and that hasn't changed. Carl-Yves kept us on edge, close to things that were happening. His beliefs pushed us. It was good to be reminded. He's a brilliant guy and he almost made me dislike him. It was Lydia's idea to look out beyond our own productions and think about distributing videos. So that idea shaped a whole new direction for VidPop. I think it kept us from becoming too insular and even from imploding. I'm not giving myself the best part here, but I think my way has been to hold things together. I'm not saying that VidPop would have exploded if I hadn't been there. I'm saying that I tend to understand what people are saying. I could see all sides.

Somehow, we fit. And then we didn't. But VidPop is not just about the four of us. I'm almost sixty-three. It's not the same as it was, this idea of retiring. Not that I can retire. And live on what? But I don't feel the need to. I'm not so worn out from work. That's one great thing about all of this. I mean I have bad patches like everyone but I still love what I do.

Lately I've been surprised by my reflection. Who is that old guy? It didn't happen suddenly but it seems a bit much somehow. I feel that I'm just now getting things right. And when I think that and feel all content, the feeling passes.

You know that moment in *La règle du jeu* by Jean Renoir, when Octave, played by Renoir himself, looks in the mirror and sees himself? He sees the ridiculousness of what he is about to do. I mean, I don't feel that way, but that look...

LISA HARROW When Maurice left, for me it was no big thing. I wasn't invested in that mythical first space, the one on lower St-Laurent. I hadn't known it. I helped with the move to the Berri Street location. I volunteered to drive small stuff over in my car. Terry was getting on my nerves a bit because it was like I was carrying artifacts or priceless objects. Lydia and some board members had prepared the move by going through papers and items and deciding what should be kept. Terry wanted to keep everything.

MARIE CHEVRIER I would have taken Maurice in but it was better for him that I went to his place instead. His sister Danielle was taking care of him, too. Danielle and I convinced him...tricked him, really, into seeing a doctor, then he was referred to a psychiatrist. He had luck with the shrink, he got someone who seemed right for him. VidPop had been his life and when he wasn't going there anymore he just felt so anxious. It was like being there at VidPop had held things together for him. It took quite some time. We would go out for short walks, go to the video store, sit on park benches and sometimes we would have a little something to eat in a café. When he and Marcel freed the machines from VidPop — I'm using Maurice's own words — when the machines were at his apartment, he set everything up as close as posssible to resemble what he knew. That made a huge difference for him. And then he started working. When I visit him, he makes me fresh orange juice with the old manual juicer from his mother and shows me what he's been up to. Once a week, we walk our dogs together.
   I ran into someone from the old days. I want to say Roland but I'm not sure. He worked in radio. Anyhow he had heard a rumor that Maurice was a recluse and a

hoarder. I don't like talking about Maurice to people unless they are close to him. There is enough shit out there about Maurice. But I said to him that he had it completely wrong. Mind you, Maurice is a bit of a recluse, but he has a lot of friends. He is also a bit of a hoarder but only for machines and videotapes. And they are kept neatly piled. It's not like those shows where you have to walk along corridors of stacked newspapers.

LYDIA CARTWRIGHT I wish I had the perfect thing to say. I've actually been thinking about it but can't come up with anything that doesn't sound completely ridiculous and pompous.

Those guys made me laugh. They also made me furious. Egos. Carl thought he could save the world maybe and when he didn't and couldn't he took it out on the rest of us. Terry sacrificed himself in some ways. I've told him this, the propensity for martyrdom. I feel bad thinking this about Maurice, knowing what we do. He was unwell. But an ego, too, thinking that his work meant more than anything else. I won't leave myself out even though I rather would. Three men and one woman at first. In the seventies! I probably thought I was the feminist conscience. I'm sure I thought that, at least some of the time. And I also thought I was so great, co-existing with those three guys.

Now I'm seeing videos and performances that are referencing older works from the seventies and eighties. It is interesting to see that ideas come around again.

I met with Nancy at the centre. She wanted to ask me questions about my work. We watched a few of my tapes together. I kind of watched some parts through my fingers, almost like when I see scary films. I have a hard time watching myself. It isn't the age thing...although my hands seem to be covered in age spots and fine black hair, which weren't there a few years ago. It's a whole different person, a different perspective, everything. When I see those works, I sometimes think 'what's she going to do next?' She. It's me. I have to fight feeling nostalgic about those videos and that place. I just have to remember something like funding cuts or someone we knew dying or the whole shattering and trying to regroup to shake myself out of wistfulness. My daughter thinks those tapes are hilarious. I tell her that in ten years, she will think they are seminal.

When Nancy curates her programs for the anniversary screenings, maybe our old work will all seem fresh and new. Terry called me and Rosemary to say that the curator who supposedly freaked out on him about Maurice's work, Neal, is coming to VidPop soon. He wants Ro and I to go and hear the story directly from him.

I've decided to send Carl-Yves something. I took a napkin, put ketchup and mustard on it, some oil. Then I wrote some words on it.

CARL-YVES DUBÉ I don't think I could sum up my experience. I'm sure Terrence will take a stab at it, though. This one was like this, this one was like that, this was the glue that held them all together...The visionary, the socialist, the intellectual, the man of the people. Or the crackpot, the pugilist, the feminist and the good guy. We should have taped everything we ever did. That would have been one way for us to agree on what actually happened.

When the record player was taken away, I kind of thought that was it. It belonged to Terrence. The music stopped. I could be such an asshole.

He found me. Terrence. For the first time in years, I got a letter. On the envelope, Vidéo Populaire. I don't think I opened it for days. I was afraid. I did actually think that Terrence might have written me a long letter or something. It was a distribution report, all the places my videos had played. And a cheque. The amount was kind of amazing. Almost three thousand dollars accumulated over the several years that I didn't let Vidéo Populaire know my whereabouts. Believe me, that is big money in independent video. I almost called Terrence because it was obvious someone was doing a very good job getting those old things into university collections. *Le travail* was still out there.

I almost called also because he had restrained himself and hadn't written a long letter begging me to get in touch. I have stayed away from Facebook.

For the 35th anniversary of Vidéo Populaire, there was a story in one of the weeklies. There they were, Terrence and Lydia in a photograph. I'm not sure I would have recognized them on the street, but then I've aged too of course. My name and Maurice's were right alongside theirs in the opening paragraph. Terrence and Lydia have always been decent about the beginning era. They credit people. That counts. Terrence seems to go too far, dragging up names I don't even recall.

I remember towards the end of my time there, Maurice had his long hair and I had decided no, that was over for me. I got my hair cut and had it short for the first time in probably a decade. Do you know what I thought at the time? It was a serious haircut for a serious revolution.

Terrence always insisted on throwing Vidéo Populaire New Year's Eve parties. We did that every year I was there and after I left the tradition continued, I think. I mean at first those parties were fun and everyone wanted to get invited. I guess we were the cool place for a while. I don't know, I have this image in my head of the 1999 New Year's Eve party, Terry standing alone, so sad, but I have no idea if that's even true. My wife told me I was just being mean. She also said that if I was still thinking things like that in 2000, she was going to force me to go to Vidéo Populaire and bury the hatchet. It isn't even about burying anything.

My kid seems to be a lot like me when I was young. He's in a band with some guys from his university. Sometimes they rehearse in the apartment. I can hear him shouting at his friends. And my wife will ask me, 'Remind you of anyone?'

I can still feel a sliver of the feeling. I wanted to tear Vidéo Populaire down. I wanted them to change the name because it was our name, we chose it and there was no 'we' anymore. I didn't want any of the equipment used unless it was for political causes. I wanted to kick certain members out. I could not be reasoned with. Terrence stood up to me. Maurice stood up to me! Lydia, too. For the first time, Terrence kicked me out. He told me to come back when I had cooled down. When I could be civil. I had made him blow up. It was obviously my exit. I'd managed to turn three people into versions of themselves that were not remotely part of their personalities. I never really cooled down. I just started to let it leak out. For years I dreamt of mont Royal exploding. Bam, blowing up the Plateau, Mile-End and downtown Montréal and scattering most of it into the St-Laurent and Vidéo Populaire with it. I'd read somewhere that mont Royal had once been a volcano.

PIERRE NADEAU   Carl's hair. It was amazing. He had mounds of curly dark hair down past his shoulders. RGB was the reason he finally cut it all off and shaved his beard, too. RGB was going around telling people Carl looked like Louis XIV. That was about the worst thing you could have told Carl, to compare him to a monarch. RGB undermined him when he could.

ROBERT T. ROBERTS   I tried to make videos and films. I couldn't. After *Dream One* I came up with another proposal and sent it to VidPop and it got accepted. I don't know how to describe it, but I couldn't do a thing. I tried very hard. I shot a bunch of stuff. I started to edit but everything looked dumb to me. I started reading about all these artists who had early success and, boom, they were done. I had endless coffees and beer with Terry and sometimes Lydia. Guy changed his name to Serge around that time. We stayed friends. Serge suggested I could help him with one of his documentaries, as a way of moving me out of my creative block. I was kind of desperate. So I stopped. I was surrounded by all these good videos in the space, all these ghosts and I got haunted, that's how I explain it. I paint now. I'm a painter who made one video, which I think is better than a video artist who did one painting.

ANTONIO DUTTO   I'm trying to wear Carl down with kindness. He never snaps at me. Possibly because he thinks on some level I'm the same naive American he met all those years ago. I don't care. I'll use that. So I keep bringing it up, VidPop. This summer I'm working on my last collaboration with my brother. I've asked Carl to help me because I can't do it myself, it's too raw. I have all of this footage Joe and I shot over the years that still might have something in it. Something elusive. Maybe it's nothing, but Carl will tell me straight out whether there is something there or not. I need to look at those images but I don't want to be alone. This project has always been me and Joe. And Joe went over his ideas with me. I have them written down. Carl doesn't know it yet but he is involved. My plan is to go to Montréal for a few weeks. I plan on visiting with Terry and Lydia. I hope to see Maurice.

DAVID SUMMERVILLE   Oh, I can do nostalgia. I can do it with the best of them. Better even.

I've told this to Lydia and Terry many times...I love them dearly but for Pete's sake just bundle Maurice up in a car and drive him over to Carl-Yves's house. They seem so... entrenched in what happened a long time ago. I can't figure out if it's out of respect or fear. Just go already.

ROSEMARY DRUMMOND   Carl-Yves deserves his due. He was instrumental. But he was there for seven years. And he never participated in any way after that. Perspective, that's what's missing from all this boo-hooing about the old days. I'm guilty of it, too. Lydia talked to me about the anniversary video — would I consider doing a proposal? I'd rather poke my own eye out. I can't imagine wanting to get in the middle of all that. I would love to watch the process, though.

LYDIA CARTWRIGHT   I'm beginning to think that Antonio is the best choice to do a video on Vidéo Populaire. Would it fly? He is American and there are many homegrown candidates. I am being strategic here. If one good thing could come of this, it would be to get Carl and Maurice back in touch. I would love to see Carl again. Terry would, too, but we're secondary. We got him out of our systems on some level. I've heard Maurice say VidPop is the past. I'm sure he believes that, surrounded by obsolete technology and video formats. It's like he moved VidPop circa 1985 to his apartment.

PIERRE NADEAU There was something there. Who knows now if it is just nostalgia speaking, but I'm happy I had that for a while. The conviction of being right and doing good. The four of them were huge influences on me, sometimes bad but overall good. I wonder sometimes if I'm not experiencing that thing where old memories seem clearer than what happened yesterday?

MAURICE AUBERT If Terry and Lydia come to my door and walked me over to the new space, maybe I could go. If Carl came over here and walked with me I would be able to for sure.

Then I wonder if I won't just make a video for the screening instead of trying to show up. Ask to have it shown at the beginning or the end of the program. I'm interested right now in using images from back then. I have shots of the three of them in the seventies. Those images are so ghostly now. They were kind of like spectres then, black and white and indistinct, but now...I don't remember the exact context but they are all just doing stuff in the first real office we had, unpacking things. It isn't long but there they are. I'm even in it for a second. Carl walks over to me and takes the camera, still rolling, and turns it on me. That weird movement where you pass a camera to someone else and they adjust it and get comfortable. I'm young. My hair is long. I'm smoking. I make this stupid smirk face. Then I'm gone. Carl turns the camera away from me to capture the new space. The movement. I have to decide if I use the images as they are. Or if I play with them in some way, maybe with some of the old signal attacking processes. Maybe just as they are. I go back and forth. Carl is the angel on my shoulder yelling 'no, don't do it, don't fuck with the images' and on my other shoulder is a little devil that looks like me saying 'do it.'

I have been thinking of Laurent. His images and voice are here. He stopped there in black and white. It's like his aging process took place on the tape. Not quite Dorian Gray. I've been thinking of him because I feel like I've been keeping him from the world, locked up. I mean he's out there. People read him. He matters. This used to be just Carl and me, knowing about it. I think we should let him go but I'm not sure how yet. I wrote something down on old VidPop letterhead. I wrote 'Cher Carl-Yves, est-ce que je devrais laisser partir Laurent?' He'll know.

I have to concentrate and fasten without fixing on a point, keeping objects blurry. I wear glasses, it's probably easier for me, I can't see far, blurry is natural, things appear to shimmer, then I can sometimes see a point that seems clear. If I can get in there, extend that point, I might come out with something I can use in a video.

TERRENCE O'MEARA We made two videos all of us together. After that, we collaborated in different ways. I would do camera for Lydia. She would help me edit my videos. Carl-Yves and Maurice basically teamed up for quite a while. We were all over each other's work. Constantly.

The videos are *Vidéo Populaire* and *Vidéo-poème pour le Québec*. 1975 and 1976. And the credits read *Une production et création de Vidéo Populaire*. Gosh. Those titles. Anyhow, they reflect the times. The idea was that we were equal in the creative process. Each one of us shot footage. Each one of us edited a sequence. For many years, I didn't show them. To be honest, for a few years there I didn't think they were all that good. But now if I'm invited to present a selection of work from VidPop, I'll have *Vidéo-poème pour le Québec* play first. We shot and shot, over six months. We did a shot where each of us is revealed in close-up after a swish pan.

The shots of us are very quick. I talk a lot about Maurice and his work, how it seems like his videos are stamped by something that gets released into the atmosphere. In *Vidéo-poème* even people who were born after 1999 can sense the giddiness we had. We took the camera on a toboggan. We hung out of a car. We did that quintessential Montréal shot on top of mont Royal shooting towards downtown. We went in a bar on St-Denis, on Saint-Jean-Baptiste, and the camera glides around and dips because everyone is singing and dancing. Including us. We practically run across pont Jacques-Cartier in traffic. You can feel our excitement. Here we go.

Participants

NANCY AMIOT (b. 1968) Independent curator and writer.

DANIELLE AUBERT (b. 1957) President and CEO of Aubert Inc., a software company. Sister of Maurice Aubert.

MAURICE AUBERT (b. 1952) One of the four founders of Vidéo Populaire. His video series *No 1* through *No 23* have been presented in festivals, universities and galleries around the world.

MYLÈNE BOISJOLI (b. 1951) Actress. Boisjoli has had a long career on the stage and has also appeared in Québec and Canadian television and film productions.

GUILLAUME R. BOIVIN (b. 1954) Aka RGB. Video producer and editor.

DAN BRISEBOIS (b. 1951) Owner and operator of Construction D. Brisebois et fils. His stands for machines created by Maurice Aubert can be seen at Vidéo Populaire.

BEVERLY CAMPBELL (b. 1965) Distribution Coordinator at Vidéo Populaire from 1997 — 2000.

LOUIS CARON (b. 1953) Owner of Taxi Caron. Caron was an early member of Vidéo Populaire.

LYDIA CARTWRIGHT (b. 1953) Video and performance artist who has taught at Concordia University since 1986. Founding member of Vidéo Populaire.

MARIE CHEVRIER (b. 1951) Freelance journalist.

NORMAND CÔTÉ (b. 1954) Video and filmmaker. Among his works are *C'est assez* (1984) and *Terre inconnue* (2004).

RÉAL COUTU (b. 1951) Worked in social services. Retired. Coutu was a board member of Vidéo Populaire from 1978 — 1985.

ROGER CROSS (b. 1963) Works as a political consultant. Cross was Distribution Coordinator at Vidéo Populaire from 1989 — 1994.

ANDRÉ CYR (b. 1955) Journalist and writer.

MARC DELORME (b. 1957) Distributon coordinator, 1978 — 1981.

ROSEMARY DRUMMOND (b. 1950) Film, video and performance artist. Well-known for her documentary portraits of female artists, *As She Is, so She Is.*

CARL-YVES DUBÉ (b. 1951) One of the four founding members of Vidéo Populaire. His documentaries *Le travail* and *L'usine* are considered classics. He currently teaches at cégep Bois-de-Boulogne.

ANTONIO DUTTO (b. 1952) Video artist and teacher. Primarily known for a series he co-directed with his brother Giuseppe 'Joe' Dutto, *The Time Has Come* (1978 — 1992).

SERGE DUVAL (b. 1948) Born Guy Ostiguy. Documentary filmmaker.

CÉCILE GRONDIN (b. 1953) Accountant. Board member of Vidéo Populaire, 1978 — 1985.

AMANDA FORSYTHE (b. 1976) Distribution Coordinator since 2009.

LISA HARROW (b. 1964) Video artist. Harrow was an active member and volunteer from 1984 — 1989.

WILLIAM JARDIN (b. 1964) Activist and social worker. Co-directed *Positive Montréal* (1991).

PHILIPPA JOHNSON (b. 1954) Social worker.

ROSAIRE LACHANCE (b. 1950) Radio personality, retired.

SERGE MASSON (b. 1952) Proprietor of Masson Électroniques.

ISABELLE MERCIER-LALONDE (b. 1954) Union president.

TERRENCE O'MEARA (b. 1950) Founding artist-member of Vidéo Populaire and current Coordinator. O'Meara teaches courses in video production at Concordia University and at Université du Québec à Montréal.

PIERRE NADEAU (1953) Editor. Made videos in the early part of his career. Also teaches at cégep André-Laurendeau.

DR. TIMOTHY PETERSON (b. 1949) Dentist.

ROBERT T. ROBERTS (b. 1962) Painter whose works are featured in the collections of several museums. Teaches at Queen's University (Kingston).

MICHEL ROBITAILLE (1965 — 1991) Co-director of *Positive Montréal*.

LORENZO SEPÚLVEDA (b. 1955) Documentary filmmaker and editor. Sepúlveda has directed twelve documentary films, including *Nation Building* (2005). He also works as an editor for fiction and documentary projects.

LUISA SEPÚLVEDA (b. 1956) Documentary filmmaker and researcher. Among her works are *Départ pour le Chili* (1994), co-directed with Lorenzo Sepúlveda, and *Pinochet* (2008).

LAURENT SIMARD (1954 — 1975) Poet and writer. His work *Cahiers* was published posthumously.

ELSA SMITH (b. 1961) Director of *La galerie juste là*. Smith was employed at Vidéo Populaire from 1982 — 1983.

MICHAEL STIRKIN (b. 1951) Lawyer. Bienville, Stirkin et Associés.

DAVID SUMMERVILLE (b. 1958) Performance and video artist. Summerville served on the Vidéo Populaire board from 1987 — 1990 and from 1995 — 1996. He also worked at VP in a variety of capacitities from 1981 — 1993.

ACKNOWLEDGEMENTS

All my gratitude to family and friends.

I thank the video artists whose work I love.
There are too many to mention.

I thank those who have written eloquently about
the video medium, its history and specificity.

Thank you, Beth Follett, for your expert
guidance. Thank you, Zab, for the beautiful
design of this book.

Merci Petunia pour ta complicité.

Merci au Groupe Intervention Vidéo.

ANNE GOLDEN is an independent curator and writer whose programs have been presented at Musée national du Québec, Edges Festival and Queer City Cinema, among others. She has written for *Fuse* and *Canadian Theatre Review*. Golden has participated in numerous panels on curatorial practices, independent distribution and, more recently, horror films. Golden is Artistic Director of Groupe Intervention Vidéo (GIV). She has made twenty videos including *Fat Chance* (1994), *Big Girl Town* (1998), *From the Archives of Vidéo Populaire* (2007) and *The Shack* (2013).